HEARTSIDE
BAY

THE **HEARTSIDE BAY** SERIES

HEARTSIDE BAY

Summer of Secrets

CATHY COLE

SCHOLASTIC

Scholastic Children's Books
An imprint of Scholastic Ltd
Euston House, 24 Eversholt Street, London, NW1 1DB, UK
Registered office: Westfield Road, Southam, Warwickshire, CV47 0RA
SCHOLASTIC and associated logos are trademarks and/or
registered trademarks of Scholastic Inc.

First published in the UK by Scholastic Ltd, 2014

Text copyright © Scholastic Ltd, 2014

ISBN 978 1407 14053 7

A CIP catalogue record for this book
is available from the British Library.

Printed by CPI Group (UK) Ltd, Croydon, CR0 4YY
Papers used by Scholastic Children's Books are made
from wood grown in sustainable forests.

1 3 5 7 9 10 8 6 4 2

www.scholastic.co.uk

An infinite number of thank yous
to Lucy Courtenay and Sara Grant

ONE

The morning sun was creeping over the window sill. A gentle breeze was blowing the curtains back against the wall. Birds sang and twittered from the branches in the tree outside.

Rhi hunched her head a little further into her shoulders and willed herself to take in something – anything – from the page of geography revision notes in front of her. She'd been staring at it for half an hour already, but none of it was sinking in. In a fit of frustration, she ripped the page from her folder and crumpled it in her fist, then threw it hard across her room where it bounced off the wall and into the waste-paper basket. The birds outside sang on, oblivious.

If those birds don't stop, I am going to do something I might regret, she thought.

She had so much to do, and so little time in which to do it. The more she thought about her exams starting on Monday, the more paralysed she felt. And the more paralysed she felt, the closer Monday came. It was a vicious circle. Her parents – her mother in particular – were depending on her to do well. Her family had been through so much in the past few years. Rhi couldn't put more stress on to the family by failing her exams.

She was already regretting crumpling the piece of paper. Fetching the creased ball from the waste-paper basket, she smoothed it out as best she could. Irrigation systems in East Anglia. Picking up a pen, she copied out the information. Maybe some of the facts would stick to her brain the same way the ink stuck to the new sheet of paper.

It didn't seem to work. Her notes still felt like a meaningless jumble of letters, numbers, arrows, boxes, graphs . . . her head hurt just looking at them. How was she ever going to remember this stuff?

This is a disaster, she thought in panic. *These exams start in just forty-eight hours and I hardly know a thing. I'm going to fail everything and Mum is going to kill me.*

Paralysis was setting in again. She slammed down her pen and shoved violently at the notes in front of her. They teetered for a moment on the edge of the desk before scattering across the carpet.

She pushed her chair back, resting the heels of her hands against her eyes. She wanted all this to *stop*.

Rhi remembered how once, as a child, she had stood perfectly still in the middle of the stairs, believing that if she stopped moving, bedtime would never come. The feeling of control had been powerful. But then her parents had started one of their arguments, and Ruth had put her head out of her bedroom door and laughed at Rhi on the stairs, and Rhi had noticed the second hand on the hall clock was still ticking. The sense of power passed. Nothing was going to stop. Time had a habit of moving on whether you wanted it to or not.

Wearily she took her hands away from her eyes, got off her chair and started picking up the mess she had created. Geography in one pile, maths in another. English, history. . .

She paused as her fingers met something she didn't

recognize. She lifted an envelope from the carpet and stared at it in surprise. It was a letter, addressed to her, with a London postmark.

It must have arrived in yesterday's post, she thought, turning it over curiously. She guessed her mother had left it on her desk, where it had been covered up by her messy revision notes. Until now.

No one wrote personal letters these days. She couldn't remember the last time she'd had a handwritten envelope in her hand. Maybe a Valentine's card from Max. It was interesting how the thought of Max didn't bother her the way it used to.

Glad of the distraction, Rhi ripped open the envelope. She had barely started reading it when she dropped it as if the paper had burned her.

It was from Mac.

A hundred thoughts tumbled through Rhi's head. Why was Mac writing to her now? What did he want? How *dare* he put pen to paper, after everything that happened? Her whole body was trembling from the shock of seeing his name. *I want nothing to do with him ever again.*

She squeezed her eyes shut, trying and failing to

blank out the memory of the last time she'd seen Christopher McAllister. The closed door that she had opened so unthinkingly. The shock on Ruth's face. Everything that had happened on that terrible day had been his fault.

Not everything, whispered the mocking voice in her head.

Don't think about it, Rhi ordered herself. *You can't change the past.*

The old, familiar wave of guilt, anger and grief welled up inside her. She stared at the letter on the carpet like it was a venomous spider. It had woken something ugly inside her and she didn't want to touch it.

Downstairs, the front door slammed so hard that the walls of Rhi's bedroom shook.

"I should have known you were planning something like this!"

Rhi's father sounded weary. "Anita, I was going to tell you—"

"How *convenient* of you not to get around to it until I found out for myself, Patrick! You really are a spineless—"

Rhi pressed her hands tightly to her ears. On top of her panic about the exams and the ice-cold shock of Mac's letter, the last thing she needed this morning was one of her parents' shouting matches. It had been particularly bad over the past few days. Rhi hardly dared to wonder what the argument was about this time.

She could still hear her mother through her fingers.

"That is *it*, Patrick. This time I've had it with—"

Sometimes her parents didn't even need a reason to argue. Her mother always raised her voice higher than her dad. *As if by shouting louder, she can block out his existence*, Rhi thought wearily, pulling her hands from her ears. There was no point in trying to block it out.

She suddenly realized that her mother was at the top of the stairs. Instinctively, Rhi dived for the letter. If her mother came in and saw who had been writing to her. . . It didn't bear thinking about.

"You always think about what's best for you, don't you Patrick? All these years I've slaved to keep food on the table for this family, and this is the thanks I get. I gave you the best years of my life—'

Trying not to look at the spidery writing on the

paper, Rhi shoved the letter back inside its envelope. She couldn't put it in the bin – her mother would see it, and open it. It was a miracle the letter had reached her unopened to begin with. So what was she going to do with it?

Her door handle turned with alarming speed. Rhi just had time to hurl herself towards her bed and stuff the letter under her pillow before her mother flung open the door.

She had a sinking feeling that she was too late.

TWO

"Maybe you can talk some sense into your father," Rhi's mother hissed, red-faced and angry in the bedroom doorway. "Because I certainly can't."

Rhi's heart rate slowed to a more manageable pace. Somehow her mother's eagle eyes had failed to see her hiding Mac's letter. She composed her face so that she looked as neutral as possible. She'd had a lot of practice.

"Talk some sense into him about what?" she asked.

"You and your father have always had your little secrets," her mother said, pointing accusingly at Rhi. "Did you know about this?"

Rhi realized with some shock that her mother's eyes were red around the edges. Had she been crying? Her mother never cried. Dr Anita Wills kept her cool at all times.

"Mum, calm down—" she began, rising from the bed.

"*Don't* tell me to calm down." Rhi's mother stalked feverishly up and down Rhi's bedroom, straightening the books on her shelves. She didn't even glance at the mess of paper on the carpet. "This is my *life*, and I'm always the last to know. Tell me the truth. *Did you know*?"

Her mother was starting to worry Rhi now. Had she completely lost it?

"I honestly don't know what you mean, Mum," she tried. "What—"

"Your father is moving out," her mother spat.

Rhi's world narrowed to a pinpoint of nothing. She couldn't believe what her mother had just said. Her parents' fighting had always been bad, but this was beyond her worst nightmares. Her father couldn't go. He couldn't leave her here.

"W . . . what?" she croaked.

"You heard me," said her mother bitterly. "He's going. Packing his bags and flitting off to Dreamland, where he has no responsibilities to his family and bills are paid with thin air. What do you think about *that*?"

The bedroom door banged open for a second time. It was unlike Rhi's father to get angry, but right now, he looked like a snorting bull. A bull, Rhi noted with a further flash of horror, that was holding a suitcase.

"What do you think you're doing, Anita?" he hissed. "We were going to tell Rhi calmly over dinner, or had you forgotten? You can be incredibly selfish, can't you?"

Her mother swelled like a balloon. "*I* can be selfish? Oh, that's rich coming from you! I have slaved for years to keep this family safe. To keep you all secure! Or those of you I have left, anyway. . ."

Rhi wanted to curl into a ball, hide under the bed – anything to make this go away.

"You're scaring her, Anita! Listen to yourself for once. Rhi, baby, listen to me. . ." Her dad was sat on the bed now, trying to comfort her. "This isn't about you, darling, it—"

"Of course it's about her!" her mother shouted. "It's about all of us!"

Rhi stared dumbly at her father as he pulled her into a hug. "Baby, I'm not going far," he said into her hair.

"I've taken a little flat near the Heartbeat Café. You can come and stay any time you like, there's a little spare room you can have. Will you do that?"

"An artist's garret," her mother snorted. "Cold, dirty, dingy, damp. You'd have our daughter there, would you? That is *so* like you, Patrick. One day you'll wake up and realize that the world doesn't turn on canvas and oil paint! One day you'll come to your senses. You'll beg me to take you back and save you from destitution. But guess what? If you leave this house, you will never be welcome here again. *Never*!"

"I promise you, Rhi," her father said gently, "everything's going to be fine. I've started painting again. I've even sold a few pieces. I can't do that in this house, you know that. I'm stifled here. I have been for years."

"This house stifles you, does it?" said Rhi's mother shrilly. "You ungrateful—"

Over her father's shoulder Rhi could see her guitar propped up against the wall of her bedroom. She felt as if she hadn't played it for ages, even though it had only been a couple of days. Now more than ever, her fingers itched to brush her guitar strings. She knew exactly what her father meant about feeling stifled. She felt stifled too.

Her music had always been a refuge from the difficulties in her life – and it felt like there had been a *lot* of difficulties. Her mother had never understood her passion, dismissing it as "a phase". But it wasn't a phase. It was *everything* to her.

Rhi had always written songs, but she had only recently started performing in public. And then she had met Brody Baxter. Brody with his fruit-stickered guitar and sapphire-blue eyes, his long tousled blond hair and his gorgeous smile. From the first moment they had sung together, Rhi had felt their connection. It had been magic. Now Rhi spent every spare moment of her time writing songs with her sister's old guitar, and practising them with Brody. They played a regular gig at the Heartbeat together, made recordings, and performed at weddings. They had a wedding that very afternoon, which was part of the reason Rhi had been up early to fit in her revision. She and Brody often talked about a future making music together. It was one of the best things in her life. It would be a career with a hundred ups and downs – Rhi knew that. Even getting this far hadn't been easy. But she knew that she wouldn't be truly happy without music in her life.

Her mother didn't understand. She wasn't a fan of anything beyond A-grades in sensible subjects that would get Rhi a sensible job.

She doesn't have the imagination to see any further than that, Rhi thought bitterly. Her father had plenty of imagination. Too much sometimes, maybe. But at least he had dreams.

She tried to say something, but the words weren't coming out.

Her parents were still shouting at each other.

"I'm sick and tired of paying for your ridiculous dreams! We still have a daughter, Patrick. Doesn't she matter to you? You've already packed your bag, so get out," Rhi's mother hissed, "before I do something I regret!"

"I already did something I regret. I married *you*!"

Her father's words stabbed Rhi through the heart.

"Stop it!" she screamed. Her parents looked round, startled. "Stop it, stop it, stop it! Why do you have to fight all the time? Do you have any idea how it feels to listen to you? To be *regretted*?"

Her father looked horrified. "Rhi, I didn't mean—"

Rhi felt as if a dam had burst inside her. "You are ripping me in half!" she shouted. "I won't be put in the middle any more, I won't. Sort it out or hate each other for ever, I don't care. Just stop making this house your battlefield!"

And she snatched up her guitar and ran out of the room, blinded by her tears.

THREE

Dimly, Rhi heard her parents shouting for her to come back as she rushed down the stairs. She wouldn't listen to them. She was *sick* of listening to them. She focused instead on grabbing a jacket from the hallstand and getting out of the front door as fast as she could. Her guitar bumped on her back as she slung it awkwardly over her shoulder. Then she started running down the street.

It was downhill all the way to the town centre from her house. The wind from the sea blew hard in her face, drying her tears as she ran. The streets were treacherous here, with cobbles and kerbs to catch unwary feet, but Rhi flew like she had wings, letting the air fill her lungs and blow away the horror of what had just happened.

She had made no conscious plans to head for the Heartbeat. And yet, ten minutes later, with her ribs aching and a stitch in her side, somehow that's where she ended up. She was glad. Everything would be OK at the Heartbeat because Brody would be there. They would sing together and, for a moment, nothing else would matter.

She collapsed against the wall beside the café's wooden door, her lungs heaving and her hair stuck in sweaty strands on her forehead. Her father's words rang through her head like a funeral bell. *I already did something I regret. I married you.*

This was it, then, she thought dumbly, sliding down the wall to the pavement as she caught her breath. The thing she had come to dread so much was finally here. Her parents were splitting up for good.

The café door opened.

"Hey," said Brody with a smile.

Rhi looked up at him with red eyes. His expression changed.

"Rhi, are you OK? What's happened?"

"Everything," she said wearily. She had no energy to get back to her feet.

Reaching out his hands, Brody pulled her up. His hands were warm, calloused from his guitar strings. "What were you running away from?"

Had she been running away from home, or running *towards* Brody? Rhi suddenly wasn't sure. Brody made her feel . . . safe, she supposed. But more than that: he made her feel whole. It scared her and thrilled her at the same time.

Brody was looking over her shoulder. "I can't see any bogeymen," he said. "No wild dogs or angry police officers either."

"I'm running away from my own head," Rhi said shakily.

Brody pulled her into a hug. "I like your head," he said against her cheek. "Your body would look very strange without it."

Rhi closed her eyes and rested her face against his shoulder. He felt warm and solid. Waves of calm were already sweeping over her, soothing her aching heart. The connection that she and Brody had formed while writing songs and performing together was something truly special. But it went beyond the music. They both knew that.

Rhi felt a shiver run through her as she remembered the single kiss she and Brody had shared. It had been electrifying. But they had agreed that a relationship might damage their professional partnership, and Rhi was determined not to do that. It had to be about the music, and nothing else.

That's what Rhi's head told her. Her heart saw things a little differently. Rhi wanted more than anything to kiss Brody again; to forget every logical reason not to fall in love with him. She was already halfway there.

"Come on," he said, pulling away from her. "We have work to do – namely an entire playlist to put together by two o'clock this afternoon. Are you up to it?"

Rhi suppressed her acute disappointment. "Of course. What's the theme?"

"Sixties peace and love. It's a great period for music. Lots of acoustic guitar in straightforward keys. It shouldn't be a problem. We might even fit in some songwriting of our own."

"I could use some extra peace and love in my life right now," Rhi said with a laugh. She plastered a smile on her face, unhooking her guitar. "Lead the way."

She and Brody had been working together with

their music so much that Rhi's dad had turned the Heartbeat's attic space into a practice room for them both. It was Rhi's haven, with its sloping ceilings and its view of the sea. They had comfy chairs in there, and a kettle, and a generous supply of biscuits.

Rhi collapsed on one of the chairs, letting the sun warm her face through the window. "So who's getting married this time?" she asked.

"A couple of pensioners."

Rhi felt surprised. They hadn't done an older wedding before. "Seriously?"

"What's so surprising about that?" Brody laughed. "The theme should have given you a clue. Older people can find love too, you know. It's at the Grand Hotel this afternoon."

Rhi felt tears blurring her eyes. "That's nice," she said, a little squeakily.

A frown appeared on Brody's face. "Something's wrong, isn't it? Don't deny it, I know you too well."

He did know her well, Rhi thought. Singing with someone, baring your soul day in, day out – it gave away your secrets a lot more than just plain friendship.

"It's my parents," she said quietly.

He grimaced. "Fighting again?"

"Worse than that. Dad's moving out."

It sounded so final, saying the words out loud. Brody looked upset.

"Rhi, I'm really sorry. That must suck."

Rhi wished he wasn't so good at listening. It made it a lot harder keeping her feelings for him under control. "They've been unhappy for years," she said, trying to shrug. "Maybe it's for the best."

Brody came to sit beside her. "Maybe. But I'm sure that's hard to understand right now."

A lot of things were hard to understand right now, Rhi thought wearily. Parents. Geography revision. Chris McAllister's letter. The guilt swept over her like burning fire again and she shivered. She hoped the letter was safe under her pillow. She would destroy it the first chance she got.

"Nothing else bothering you?"

Brody was watching her. For a moment she thought of telling him about Mac and . . . that day. The guilt was so hard to bear alone. But she dismissed the thought almost as soon as she'd had it. Brody was so good and kind. So understanding. So perfect. She couldn't expect him to understand the terrible mistake she had made.

"Just revision," she lied, rubbing her eyes with her hands. "Exams. You know. There's a lot going on right now. It's hard to concentrate."

Brody nodded, accepting her answer. "Let's sing," he said, picking up his guitar.

They spent the next hour working through the wedding playlist they'd been given. It was full of classics: Bob Dylan, Joni Mitchell, Joan Baez, Crosby Stills & Nash. Rhi gave herself over to the gentle rhythms and the poetry of the lyrics. She'd been listening to these songs since she was a small child, thanks to her father's taste in music. She knew most of the words without needing to practise them, and the chords were generally simple.

"Great," said Brody, ticking off the last song on the list: Cat Stevens' "The Wind". "Now we've done the hard stuff, want to work on some new material?"

"Sure," said Rhi, interested at once. "What did you have in mind?"

Brody retuned his guitar, plucking and turning the

pegs. "I've written a new melody. It even has a title. But I need you for the lyrics. You're my beautiful lyric queen." He smiled at her, reaching out his thumb and stroking her cheek.

Rhi felt a little thrill in the pit of her stomach as colour flooded her cheeks. The touch of his thumb . . . he'd called her beautiful. Was he flirting with her, or was this just about the music?

"I'll see what I can do," she said. "What is it called?"

"'Small Black Box'."

Rhi was intrigued. "What does it mean? What do you want the song to be about?"

Brody didn't look at her as he placed his fingers on the strings. "Secrets," he said. "The kind you might keep under lock and key in a—"

"—small black box," Rhi finished for him. Her heart was thumping uncomfortably. Had Brody read her mind? Did he know how many secrets she was keeping?

He started playing, his blond hair hanging down over his face. It was a fast, complicated rhythm, almost angry in its intensity. He played it several times for her until she got the tune fixed in her head. She could see the small black box in her mind: red lacquered interior, small silver key – devastating contents. She knew all about secrets.

She plucked out the chords she'd seen Brody play. "You might think I'm simple," she sang, feeling for the words. "You might say I'm free, but truth to tell, baby, you know nothing 'bout me."

Brody's fingers seemed to tense against the strings.

"No good?" Rhi said, stopping at once.

He shook his head. "Sorry, no. I mean – yes. It's good. Keep going."

The words were coming from somewhere deep inside Rhi. She let them flow. "You know nothing 'bout sorrow," she sang more strongly, "know little 'bout pain, those memories that pierce you again and again. . ."

One of Brody's guitar strings snapped with a harsh pinging sound, making Rhi jump. He looked annoyed with himself.

"Keep going," he said a little abruptly.

The words were almost writing themselves. Rhi surged on, her fingers falling naturally into the rhythm of the song. "Got a small black box, locked up tight, hidden the key deep in the night – a small black box, buried down deep. . ."

"Sometimes there's secrets you just have to keep."

Rhi glanced at Brody, startled. Was he adding to the lyric, or was it more than that? Her stomach flopped uncomfortably. He was looking right back at her with an expression on his face that she'd never seen before. He seemed . . . *frightened*.

"Are you OK?" she felt compelled to ask.

The look had vanished. She wondered if she'd imagined it as he looked down at his watch.

"I need to buy a new string," he said. "I have to go."

"You bought a box of them only a couple of weeks ago," Rhi pointed out.

He wouldn't meet her eye. 'I, uh – you're right, but . . . I don't seem to have them with me. I'm going to head home."

Rhi could have sworn the box of strings was in his bag. She'd seen them in there only yesterday. *It's me*, she thought with a lurch. *He knows I'm keeping something from him. . .*

24

He was almost at the door already. "See you at the Grand Hotel later."

"Brody?" Rhi said.

But he had gone.

FOUR

Numbly, Rhi listened to the sound of Brody's footsteps hurrying away down the stairs. It sounded like he was taking the steps two at a time, like he couldn't wait to get away from her.

It was the last straw in a difficult morning. Rhi burst into tears, screwing her fists into her eyes. She didn't need to be a genius to work out that she'd upset Brody. His face had looked almost waxen when he had left. She'd somehow managed to break the most precious thing in her life. The one thing that kept her sane.

He knows I'm keeping secrets. The thought made Rhi cry harder. She hated the guilt that Mac's letter had brought back. The memories. . . The terror of the impending exams. . . Her parents dropping that bombshell about her dad moving out. And now this.

I can't bear it, she thought in a mist of pain.

She cried until her eyes were red-raw.

The attic door opened.

"Rhi!"

Her dad ran across the room and put his arms around her as she gasped for breath.

"Baby, don't cry. Please don't cry. You're breaking my heart. I'm so sorry about this morning. . ." He wiped the tears from her cheeks. "I saw your music friend as he was leaving – he told me where I would find you. I should have known you'd come here, shouldn't I?"

"My life's such a mess," Rhi sobbed in his arms. When – how – had everything gone so wrong?

He stroked her hair. "You're not the only one, darling. I'm so, so sorry. You weren't supposed to find out like that. Your mother and I have tried to keep things going for your sake, but it's no good. I wish I could tell you otherwise, but it's over. The truth of it is, it's been over since before Ruth died."

Rhi hiccuped. "Since . . . before Ruth?"

"I was planning to leave in the weeks before the

accident." His eyes looked haunted as he stared at her, willing her to understand. "But . . . when it happened I couldn't do it. I felt too guilty. You needed me, and your mum . . . Well, I thought she needed me too. But it turned out that she didn't. And I can't do it any more, honey. I just can't."

He was crying too, Rhi noticed.

"I understand, Dad," she found herself saying. "Honestly, I do."

"Thank you," he said quietly.

He looked tired and old. In need of looking after. The thought of him alone while she was stuck in the house with her mother suddenly overwhelmed Rhi.

"Can I come and live with you in your new flat?" she blurted. "I can go home right now and pack and—"

"You have exams to think about," he interrupted, wiping his tears away with the backs of his hands. "My flat's a mess, Rhi. Your mother's right – it is dingy, and small, with hardly any space for you to do your work in the peace and quiet that you need. It's no place for you. You have to stay with your mother. She needs you."

Rhi felt like a punctured tyre. Her father didn't want her, it seemed.

"Mum doesn't need me," she said dully. "She needs Ruth."

Her father flinched. "That's not true."

"She always preferred Ruth." It felt liberating to say it out loud. "Ruth made more sense to her. Ruth was clever, and ambitious about all the same things Mum is ambitious about. Mum doesn't understand me like you do, Dad. *Please* can I come and live with you? I'm begging you—"

"No," her father repeated firmly. "Don't make this harder than it already is, Rhi. Home is the best place for you right now."

Rhi's eyes filled with hot tears again. "I can't believe you're deserting me!" she burst out.

He looked as if she had stabbed him through the heart. "Rhi, I'm not—"

Rhi grabbed her guitar and ran out, slamming the attic door before he could finish his sentence. She didn't want to listen to another word. He had betrayed her when she needed him most.

No one understands what it's like to be me, she thought despairingly. *No one.*

Mac's letter swam at the edges of her mind, insistent

and relentless. She headed down to the beach, suddenly desperate to be alone. Just her and the gulls and the wind in her face. She wanted the wind to scour her guilt away.

She found a niche among the rocks at the water's edge and curled up, the sand cool and a little damp beneath her. Instinctively she settled her guitar around her neck and placed her fingers on the strings. As she played the familiar chords, she felt her breathing grow easier and her mind calmer. She didn't need the wind. She needed her music.

She sang several songs, one after the other, gazing out to sea and letting her mind drift on the lyrics and the sound of the waves curling against the sand. When she was feeling calm again, she stood up and brushed the sand from her jeans. There was revision to do, and preparations to be made for that day's wedding. Life went on, whether she wanted it to or not.

She had to go home.

The house seemed empty and quiet as Rhi let herself in. She felt a little of the tension seeping out of her as she put her house keys down on the hall table. She wasn't ready to face her mother just yet. She'd had enough scenes for one day already. Having the house to herself was just what she needed. She set her guitar down at the foot of the stairs and headed for her bedroom.

Her mother swung round as Rhi opened the bedroom door. Everything seemed to stop as Rhi glimpsed the envelope from Mac's letter lying empty on the bed.

Her mother held the letter out.

"What is this, Rhi?"

Rhi was speechless. How had her mother found the letter? What was she *doing* in here? This was Rhi's private space. Did her mother make a habit of snooping around when she was out? She felt hot as she imagined the things her mother might have found and read. And now this. Her worst nightmare was coming true already.

"Rhi?" her mother repeated.

Rhi took an involuntary step towards her. "Why are you in my room?"

"You haven't answered my question." Her mother frowned down at the letter, at the spidery black writing. "Who is this boy? Why is he apologizing for hurting you?"

Rhi realized in a sudden flood of relief that her mother hadn't recognized the name at the bottom of the letter. He had always been Christopher McAllister in the court reports, in the paper. Never Mac, the name he went by in real life. She snatched the letter from her mother's fingers, scrunched it into a ball and held it close to her chest. She felt hot with anger and guilt.

"You had no right to read it," she said.

Her mother folded her arms. "I have every right. You're my daughter. If something is worrying you, if this boy has hurt you, I demand to know about it. This is an important year. You can't let anything distract you from your work."

Work, work, work. It was as if her mother was incapable of thinking about anything other than Rhi's stupid exams. As if her parents splitting up wasn't a distraction! Rhi felt such a rush of rage that, for a moment, she didn't trust herself to say anything at all.

"Why is he apologizing?" her mother repeated. "Who is he?"

"He's just someone I used to know in London,

all right?" Rhi said. She could feel her whole body shaking. "Not that it's any of your business."

Her mother frowned in annoyance. "Don't use that tone with me, Rhi. What is the matter with you at the moment? I swear, I will never understand you." She held out her hand. "Give back that letter at once."

Rhi couldn't hold it back any more.

"I understand why Dad left you!" she cried. "I wish more than anything that I could leave you too!"

The moment the words had left her lips, Rhi was wishing she could take them back. All the anger, all the rage – everything vanished in an appalling cloud of guilt. She couldn't believe she had just said something so terrible out loud.

The colour had drained from Rhi's mother's face.

"W . . . what did you say?" she whispered.

Rhi stared at her mother, aghast. "I . . . I'm sorry. I. . ."

Her mother's face seemed to crumple before Rhi's horrified gaze as she burst into tears. Rhi hadn't seen her mother cry since Ruth's funeral. This was awful.

What kind of daughter says something like that to

her own mother? she thought in horror. *Ruth would never have done anything so unkind.*

"Mum," she said, half-choked with tears herself. "I didn't mean that. I was angry, I'm really sorry . . . I didn't mean it. Honestly, I didn't. Please don't cry."

She stepped forward instinctively, to give her mother a hug. Then she stopped. Dr Anita Wills didn't do hugs. Maybe that was part of the problem, Rhi thought unhappily. How could she and her mother be such different people?

With a visible effort, Rhi's mother straightened her shoulders, and shook her head like a dog with water in its ears. "Apology accepted," she said after a moment. Her voice was unsteady. "This has been a difficult time for you. I'm sorry you had to find out about your father and me the way you did."

"I'm sorry," Rhi said again. She felt hopelessly inadequate.

Her mother gave a nod and walked out of Rhi's room, shutting the door quietly behind her. Rhi stood alone, staring at the door. That had been intense. She sank slowly on to the bed, reaching up with her hand to push her hair back from her forehead.

The paper that was still clenched in her hand crinkled. Unfolding her fingers, she smoothed the letter out on her knee.

Dear Rhi,

I'm sorry about everything. I wish you knew how sorry. I've tortured myself every day since it happened. All I want is forgiveness. I know it's a lot to ask, but I'm asking anyway. I have nothing else.

Mac

Rhi stared at the scrawled words. Mac wanted forgiveness.

Don't we all, she thought wearily.

She could barely forgive herself. How was she supposed to forgive *him*?

FIVE

Somehow it was already ten past one. Rhi roused herself with a start. The wedding started at two and she hadn't even begun to get ready. Thank goodness she and Brody had practised the playlist. Her stomach clenched uncomfortably as she remembered the strange way that Brody had made excuses and left their rehearsal that morning. They'd never parted like that before.

The tune and half-formed lyrics of "Small Black Box" played in a loop through her head as she hurriedly selected clothes from her wardrobe that would fit the wedding's sixties theme: a flowing white dress that contrasted beautifully with her coppery skin, beaded sandals and a floral headpiece that she positioned on her hair like a crown. She would have liked to paint some flowers on her face with make-up, but there wasn't time.

She still felt awful about what she'd said to her mother. It had been a tough morning, but Rhi knew that was no excuse.

Maybe she should try to talk to her again, she thought uneasily.

She headed downstairs and hesitated outside the closed study door. She could hear her mother inside, pacing from side to side, talking loudly on the phone. Further apologies would have to wait. Feeling mildly relieved, Rhi picked up her guitar and headed into the blustery afternoon.

Wedding guests were gathering in the reception area of the Grand Hotel by the time Rhi arrived. They had all stuck faithfully to the hippy theme, and were wearing an amazing assortment of velvet jackets, beaded tops, floral garlands and afghan coats that Rhi felt pretty sure were original. It was amazing to think of all these people dancing barefoot in meadows during those crazy days of the sixties when they hadn't been much older than she was.

"Rhi, you look so pretty!"

Rhi swung round to see Lila and Polly grinning at her.

"Hippy waitresses, I see," she teased, feeling happier already at the sight of her friends. It was always more fun when they ended up working at the same wedding. "I like it."

"What, this old thing?" Lila said. She smoothed down her short paisley smock and adjusted the strip of beaded suede tied around her head. "Actually," she confided, "it *is* really old, it belonged to my grandmother and smells of mothballs."

"Are all the canapés veggie?" asked Rhi, peering at the assortment of little spinach quiches and asparagus bundles on Lila and Polly's catering trays.

Polly giggled. She was looking very pretty in a long floral dress with daisies braided into her hair. "Don't tell Mr Gupta, but I've already scoffed a few in the kitchen. I didn't have time for lunch."

"Waitress?" called a very tall old gentleman in a floppy green hat with a flamboyant pink silk scarf tied around his neck. "Is this sparkling dandelion wine organic?"

"Better go," Lila giggled. "Brody will be pleased to see you, he's through there."

38

Rhi tried to steady her nerves as she shouldered through the crowd to the room at the back of the hotel where the wedding party was being held. Her stomach turned as she saw Brody by the little stage, looking gorgeous in striped linen trousers and a fringed suede waistcoat.

"Hey," he said as she approached. He sounded awkward. "I'm really sorry about running off this morning."

"Don't worry about it. Hey yourself," Rhi mumbled back. She realized she was gazing a little too intently at his tanned chest where it peeped out from beneath the suede waistcoat, and wrenched her eyes away in a fit of embarrassment. "You look very, uh, nice."

She could have kicked herself. *Nice* was a word that grannies used around their grandchildren. *Nice* wasn't how Brody looked today. *Gorgeous* was closer. He suited the hippy look.

"Thanks," he said, sounding even more awkward. "You look very nice too."

There was an odd silence.

"I hope you fixed your guitar string," Rhi blurted.

Of course he fixed his string, she thought a little

hopelessly. *I'm staring right at his guitar and all its strings are in place. What a stupid question.*

"Yeah, I did. All tuned now and ready to play if you are?"

Rhi hated this weird formality that had suddenly come between them. She wished they'd never started working on that stupid song about secrets. Somehow that was where the trouble had all started.

"So," she said, making a show of looking around in a bid to avoid his eyes. "Which two are the happy couple?"

Brody pointed across the room. A very small, bent-over couple in matching patchwork coats were sitting at one of the tables with glasses of sparkling dandelion wine in their hands. They were both smiling so happily that Rhi felt a little swoosh in her stomach.

"Do you know how they met?" she asked as the bride and groom clinked their glasses together and gazed into each other's eyes.

"Apparently they've been friends since the sixties, but only got together a couple of months ago."

Rhi was startled. "A couple of *months* ago? And they're getting married already?"

"When you know, you know," Brody said. He lifted his fingers in the classic hippy salute. "Peace and love, baby."

Peace and love. Rhi decided she could use a bit of both. She stared at the newly-weds again. *At the rate I'm going, I'll probably be seventy before I sort out my love life too*, she thought with a sigh.

"Ready to play?" Brody asked.

Rhi climbed on to the stage. Brushing against Brody's warm arm by mistake, she jumped into the air like a startled horse.

"What's this then, *Riverdance*?" called an old man in the crowd, to a friendly roar of laughter.

Rhi smiled weakly out at the crowd. She had to keep it together. The guests may have been old, but something told her they weren't going to be easy to impress.

"What's first?" she asked Brody under her breath.

"'Blowin' in the Wind'."

Rhi played and sang the harmonies just as they had practised, but she couldn't seem to find the spark she usually had with Brody when they performed together. The strange events of the morning had cast a shadow, and Rhi felt out of sync. She was trying too hard, she knew. Her best music came when she went with the flow, but that seemed beyond her today.

Halfway through their set, Rhi's eyes were drawn to a figure by the door. She couldn't see his face on account of the hat he wore, pulled low over his eyes, but his hands and his clothes suggested he was younger by at least fifty years than most of the other guests. Someone's grandson, she guessed, although he seemed to be by himself, as if he didn't know anyone else in the room. She wondered how he had come to be in a wheelchair. Perhaps he'd been that way since birth.

Life in a wheelchair in Heartside Bay must be tough, Rhi thought. The town was a mess of cobbles, steps and hills. How did he get around? Did he have to rely on other people to help him all the time? In and out of shops, on and off buses? She couldn't imagine what his life would be like.

She was so busy thinking about the mysterious boy that she almost missed her cue on the next song. Feeling flustered, she rushed the first verse, only finding her stride at the chorus. Three more songs to go. It was important that she kept her focus, for Brody's sake.

Her eyes drifted towards the boy again. Perhaps it was the effect of the chair he was sitting in, but there was something slumped and sad about the way he held himself. It didn't look as if he was having much fun. His hat was still pulled down over his eyes, but Rhi felt sure that he was watching her.

I'll find him at our first break, she thought in a fit of compassion. *I'll talk to him. He's probably desperate for some young conversation.*

A smattering of applause greeted the end of their final song. Rhi stood and bowed beside Brody. As the clapping trailed off, Rhi laid down her guitar and left the stage, pushing through the crowd towards the door where she'd seen the boy in the chair. She wasn't sure what she was going to say. She'd figure that out when she had to.

When she reached the door, she stopped and looked around, puzzled. He wasn't there.

43

SIX

"Lovely singing."

Rhi swung round. She had been so absorbed in searching the room for the boy that she hadn't noticed anyone approach. "I'm sorry?"

It was the old man in the big green hat who'd asked Lila about the dandelion wine. "I said, lovely singing," he repeated. "You remind me of a girl I met in Morocco once. What was her name now?"

Rhi hadn't seen the boy leave the room – but then again, she hadn't been watching all that carefully. She had hunted pretty much all over the hotel, and now she was due on stage again. He had clearly left the party. Rhi felt oddly disappointed. *Typical of my luck*, she thought.

"Sunrise!" the old man exclaimed.

He was even madder than he looked, Rhi decided, suppressing a giggle. "I'm sorry?" she said politely.

"Her name was Sunrise," the old man said. "Of course she was really called Anthea, but we all had silly names in those days."

Rhi discreetly checked her watch. She needed to be on stage in two minutes. "I've got to get back," she said weakly, gesturing to the stage. "Do you mind. . .?"

"Of course," said the man, and doffed his hat at her as she slid past. "Good luck with the rest of your show."

Brody was beckoning Rhi from the stage.

"Who were you looking for?" he asked curiously as she joined him again.

"No one important," Rhi said, deciding it would be too complicated to explain. "What are we starting the second set with?"

The dandelion wine was flowing freely, and the guests had started dancing. Rhi and Brody did a couple of lively numbers, but it was the quiet songs with the sweet lyrics that got the crowd going, standing up with their hands in their air and their eyes closed as they swayed like grass in the breeze. Thinking about their youth, perhaps: girls called Sunrise, and ankle bells, and Morocco.

Rhi and Brody performed two more sets before the guests began to depart, drifting arm in arm out into the early evening sun. Rhi decided she liked early weddings. It meant that she'd earned some money, but still had the whole evening to do what she liked. That probably meant revision. She winced as she thought about her revision notes still lying in an unorganized jumble on her bedroom floor. No wonder her mother found her so disappointing. Her mood, which had briefly risen through the afternoon, was in danger of dropping like a stone again.

"Earth to Rhi," said Brody in her ear.

Rhi jumped. "I . . . what?"

He looked curiously at her. "I was just saying, good work. Not our best maybe, but pretty good none the less." He nodded at the departing guests. "They all seemed to like it."

"It wasn't my best performance," Rhi said, biting her lip. "I kept losing it in the first set. I have . . . a lot on my mind."

46

Brody slung his guitar over his shoulder. "You and me both," he said, almost to himself.

This was her chance, Rhi realized. To ask Brody what had happened that morning to make him run away from her. She wasn't sure she wanted to know the answer, but it had to be better than nothing.

"Brody," she began a little hesitantly.

He spoke at the same time. "Rhi, I was thinking—"

They both stopped. Rhi smiled sheepishly.

"You first," she said.

Brody rubbed his hands through his hair. "That song we were working on this morning," he said.

Rhi's blood froze. She was right. He was going to ask her what she was keeping from him. "What about it?" she said, a little breathlessly.

"It was about secrets."

Rhi felt sick. "Yes?"

He seemed to be steeling himself. "I want to tell you—"

"Rhi, come on! Polly and I have been waiting for ages."

It took Rhi a couple of seconds to realize Lila was standing by the stage, looking expectantly at her.

"You have remembered, haven't you?" Lila said reproachfully. "About the sleepover at mine tonight?" Her gaze darted towards Brody. "You haven't arranged something else?"

Amid the stress of the day, Rhi had forgotten entirely about the plans she and her friends had made at the end of the previous week. She suddenly had a blissful vision of sitting around in a group with her girlfriends, wearing face packs, painting their toenails and talking. After the day she'd had, it was just what she needed.

"Lila, you're a genius!" she exclaimed. "I *had* forgotten, sorry – but I'm totally up for it. I'll have to go home and pack a bag, and then I'll see you at yours in about an hour. Is that OK?"

"Perfect," said Lila happily. "We haven't had a catch-up in ages. We're all so sick of revision that any conversation about schoolwork is completely banned."

"Fine by me," said Rhi with feeling.

Lila waved and disappeared through to the kitchen.

"Nice singing," said Mr Gupta, approaching them with two brown envelopes full of money. "There will be more bookings, I am sure. The guests loved you today, we've had a lot of compliments."

Pocketing her envelope, Rhi looked at Brody again. He'd been about to tell her something when Polly had appeared. *Maybe he's going to say he likes me as more than just a singing partner*, she thought with a little shiver of hope. She could dream, couldn't she?

"I didn't mean to interrupt you," she said, hoping she hadn't missed the moment. "What did you want to say?"

He slid his envelope into the top pocket of his waistcoat and adjusted his guitar on his back. "Just . . . do you want to meet tomorrow for another songwriting session?"

Rhi felt sure he had said he had something to *tell* her, not ask her.

"Uh, sure," she said slowly. "If you want."

"Great," he said. "I have lots of ideas for new songs. Usual time at the Heartbeat? See you there."

He gave her a brief hug and headed towards the door, the street and the sunshine. Rhi felt stupidly bereft.

SEVEN

"I'm thinking of going back to blonde," said Polly.

Rhi, Lila and Eve all tipped their heads to one side to consider the current shade of Polly's hair: a warm reddish brown.

"What's wrong with red hair?" Eve objected, smoothing her own auburn locks back over her shoulders. "I've had it all my life."

"For all the good it's done you," said Lila.

Eve cuffed Lila round the ear. "I'll have you know that Becca thinks it's one of my best features," she said with a pout.

"Well," said Lila seriously, "she doesn't have a lot to choose from, does she?"

Eve was notoriously difficult to tease, and only Lila

ever dared try. Rhi found herself holding her breath as Eve glared at Lila – until at the last minute she sensed the glint of playfulness in Eve's narrowed grey eyes.

"Believe me, darling," she said, "redheads have *all* the fun."

"I haven't been having much fun lately," Polly sighed, flopping back on Lila's bed. "All that revi—"

Rhi, Eve and Lila simultaneously gasped. Polly clapped her hands over her mouth.

"Forfeit!" Lila shouted, scrambling to her feet and pointing at Polly. "You said the R word. Forfeit, forfeit, forfeit!"

"Sorry!" Polly squeaked through her fingers. "I didn't mean to, it just slipped out!"

"That's what they all say," Eve observed, lolling back on the big beanbag. "What shall we make her do, girls?"

"Burst into Tim's bedroom without knocking," Lila suggested, giggling.

Polly paled. "Don't make me do that. Your brother already thinks I'm mad."

"He's only met you once, why would he think that? Ooh, wait." Lila sat up, her eyes gleaming. "I have a better idea. Knock on Tim's door and tell him you have a crush on him."

Rhi burst out laughing as Polly groaned and covered her head with her hands. Lila looked triumphant.

"Can I accept the first dare instead?" Polly begged.

"It's much too late for that," Eve said, grinning. "Go on. We all agreed that if we said the R word we'd pay the price."

Polly took a very deep breath and got to her feet. "I hate you all," she said as she walked out of Lila's room.

Rhi huddled up close with the others by the doorframe as they listened to Polly's footsteps on the landing. There was a muffled knock, and the sound of a door opening.

"She's actually doing it," Lila said, looking at Rhi and Eve with wide eyes. "I never thought Polly had it in her!"

Polly was the shyest in the group. If Rhi hadn't heard her knock with her own ears, she would never have believed Polly would rise to a challenge like this. She couldn't think of anything more mortifying. She wriggled a little further back into the room, dreading what she might overhear.

"Going out with Ollie must be improving her confidence," Lila went on. "Did either of you think she'd do it?"

"Shh," Eve said, "I'm trying to *listen*."

The three of them were almost flattened against the bedroom wall as Polly flew back into the room again with cheeks as pink as two roses.

"What did he say?" Rhi asked breathlessly. "No, don't tell me, I don't think I can stand it. . ."

"You seriously told my brother you had a crush on him?" said Lila, trying to peer around Polly towards her brother's room.

Polly went pinker. "I said what you told me to say."

"Then how come I just saw Tim walking down the street?" asked Eve, who was standing at the window. "There's no way he could have got downstairs and out of the front door between now and then."

"Oh my gosh, you *liar*," said Lila, poking Polly in the shoulder. "He wasn't in his room, was he?"

Rhi could hardly breathe for laughing. The ache in her stomach felt so good. She hadn't laughed properly for ages.

"I said it though," Polly insisted stubbornly

through the gales of laughter. "Just because he wasn't there to hear it, doesn't mean I didn't complete the forfeit."

'You're forgiven," Lila gasped, catching her breath. "But only because that was actually hilarious. Going out with Ollie suits you. I never thought you'd even knock on the door."

Polly beamed. "I still can't believe we're together. This is *Ollie* we're talking about, after all. He's like a sort of . . . god."

"Om," said Eve solemnly, putting her hands in a prayer position, and making Lila laugh all over again. "If Polly and Ollie are cute, you and Josh are just completely adorable, Lila. You can't take your eyes off each other. I don't think I've ever seen you this happy."

Lila gave a little twirl on the carpet. "And what about you and Becca?"

Eve's eyes were soft. "What about us?"

"Talk about made for each other," Polly sighed. "You're a different person now you're with her, Eve. So much . . . nicer."

Eve swatted Polly gently with a magazine, but she was smiling.

54

Rhi tried to smile too. It wasn't that she begrudged her friends their various happy relationships. It was just . . . she felt a little left out of conversations like this these days. If only she could sort out her feelings for Brody. If only he would ask her out.

"I think we should stop talking about our love lives now," said Polly, catching sight of the expression on Rhi's face.

The others looked guilty. Rhi flushed. "Oh, please don't do that," she begged. "I like hearing about you guys. You heard enough about me and Max over the years."

"Max is history," said Eve with a wave of her hand. "We're more interested in you and Guitar Hero these days. How are you getting along?"

Rhi flushed even more as all three of her friends fixed her with beady eyes.

"Brody?" she stammered. "Oh, you know. We're just friends."

"There was nothing friendly in that kiss you had when you were doing your recording a few weeks ago," Lila observed.

Rhi felt hot at the memory. It had been . . . intense.

Especially when Max had come barging in and punched Brody in the jaw. "One moment of madness," she said weakly. "He's not interested."

Lila pounced. "But you're interested in *him*."

"Yes, OK," Rhi said reluctantly. "I do like him as more than a singing partner. But I don't think he feels the same way. And anyway. . ."

I have other things to think about right now. She didn't say the words out loud. Her dad's decision to move out was still too raw to share.

"Anyway what?" said Lila.

"Nothing," Rhi muttered. Her mood was sinking rapidly.

"Rhi?" Eve put her hand on Rhi's sleeve. "We know about your dad."

Rhi looked up, startled. "You know what about my dad?"

"We know he's moved out," said Lila. "We're really sorry."

Rhi felt her mouth fall open. "But . . . how do you know that?"

Polly looked uncomfortable. "You know Mum works at the estate agents? Your dad went into her office to ask about renting a flat last week. And . . . you know. I go in his gallery a lot. We talk."

Rhi couldn't take this in. "You knew about my dad moving out before I did?"

"It's a small town," said Eve. She looked wry. "Believe me, I know all about small towns."

"And I know all about surviving divorces," said Polly. "You're going to be fine, you know. It'll be hard to begin with, but you'll get through it. I did."

"Between us, we have all the tools you need for coping," said Eve.

"Don't be mad," Lila said, watching Rhi anxiously. "We just want you to know that we're here for you. You know, if you need to talk."

"We're here even if you don't want to talk," Eve added. "Talking can be a drag sometimes."

Polly gave Rhi a tight hug. "How *are* you feeling?" she said, releasing her.

The only feeling Rhi could identify right now was gratitude. Wordlessly she held out her arms. Lila and Eve and Polly all crowded round her for a fierce group hug.

"I'm OK," she said, when she released them. "For now anyway."

"Good," said Lila with a nod. "This calls for cake."

"And ice cream," Eve added.

"And sprinkles," Polly said. "And cheesy music and some serious toenail painting."

Rhi burst out laughing. "I love you guys."

EIGHT

After only a few hours' sleep on Lila's floor, Rhi staggered outside into the Sunday morning sunshine. The others were still out cold, but Rhi had an appointment that she had no intention of missing.

She had brought her guitar with her to the sleepover. If she'd had to go back home to fetch it, she had a nasty feeling her mother would have forbidden her from leaving the house again. An image of her revision notes lying on the ground pushed into her head, and for a moment Rhi felt cold with fear at the thought of tomorrow's exams.

Maybe I should go home, she thought, hesitating. *Maybe Brody is the last person I need to be with just now.* But she couldn't make herself believe it.

He had been the first person she thought of when she had opened her eyes that morning to the sound of Eve snoring on the pull-out bed beside her. Talking about him to her friends last night had helped sort out a few things in her head. She really liked him, but if he didn't want anything to happen beyond singing, she would accept that. She wouldn't sacrifice her music for the sake of a few kisses.

Thinking about kisses instantly recalled the electrifying kiss she and Brody had briefly shared. It wasn't a helpful memory.

Why is it so hard to do the right thing? Rhi thought with a sigh.

She scrubbed at her eyes, yawning as she walked down the lane towards the Heartbeat. Shading her eyes in the bright morning light, she squinted up at the high attic windows stretching down the street between her and the Heartbeat. Her father's flat was up there somewhere. He would probably be sleeping, or maybe painting, only a few metres away from where she was standing. The thought made Rhi feel a little sick.

She suddenly caught sight of herself in a shop window. Her hands flew to her hair in horror. Half of

it was stuck to the side of her head, while the rest. . .
She couldn't even *begin* to describe the rest.

Brody definitely won't fancy you with your hair looking like this, she thought.

Fishing around in her jacket pocket, she pulled out a ribbon which she used as a headband to keep the most out-of-control bits of hair out of her face. She fluffed up the rest and looked at herself critically in the window. It had helped a little, at least. Then she hurried around the corner and pushed through the Heartbeat Café door, following the familiar sound of Brody tuning his guitar way up in their attic practice room.

"I like the hair," Brody grinned as Rhi burst into the attic.

Rhi's hands flew self-consciously to the ribbon. Not such a good job after all, then. "I know, it's awful. I was at Lila's last night and woke up kind of late. . ."

"Don't worry about it," he laughed. "I don't care what you look like."

Rhi tried not to take offence. Brody simply meant that he liked her for who she was, didn't he?

"What do you want to work on today?" she asked.

"Let's run through the set for Wednesday's gig," he suggested.

They practised the songs they had planned for their regular Heartbeat slot, working through them slowly and carefully to make sure they were all secure. Rhi did her best to sing better than she had at the previous day's wedding, but she still missed several entries and fluffed the second verse on one of her favourite songs: Brody's "Fast Lane Freak". She didn't seem able to relax into the music today.

"I have a new tune that came to me last night," Brody said after they'd been practising for a couple of hours. "No title this time. I don't even know what I want it to be about. I thought I'd let you figure that out for me."

Not "Small Black Box" *then*, Rhi thought. She had wondered if he would suggest finishing their song about secrets this morning. They'd only got a third of the way through anything resembling a decent lyric yesterday when it had all gone wrong. She felt relieved.

As Brody started playing, she found herself getting lost in the harmonies he created with his guitar. The new tune had a melancholy feeling that made her nervous. She didn't feel up to writing a sad song today.

"What do you think?" he asked as the final chord died away.

Rhi's throat felt tight. "It's beautiful," she said. "Your songs always are."

"The music isn't finished. It needs a middle section." He looked straight at her. "Are you up for it?"

The tightness in Rhi's throat threatened to get tighter. "I . . . I'll try," she said.

Her guitar felt leaden under her fingers. She strummed a few chords, tested out a couple of progressions, but it felt like she was trying to force a jigsaw piece into the wrong place.

"Let's try some lyrics," Brody suggested after ten excruciating minutes of nothing.

Rhi had to get it together. There was so much sadness in her own life, surely she could coax out a few words to match the haunting little melody that Brody was trying to build? Trying not to feel pressured, she took up a piece of paper and a pencil.

Sad, she wrote. *Bad. Glad.* Seriously, were those the

best rhymes she could come up with? She had to do better than that. She stared in some desperation at the blank page in front of her. *Dad.*

Her eyes blurred.

Brody looked up as she threw the pencil across the room, where it skittered and spun to a halt. "What happened?" he asked in surprise.

Rhi felt panicky. "I can't think of anything," she said. Her mind was a total blank. It was as if the free-flowing words she had created from thin air the morning before had never happened.

He set his guitar down. "Are you feeling OK?"

Rhi stared at the three words she'd written. It felt as if there were no words left inside her at all. And, if her lame attempt at writing the middle section was anything to go by, no music either. She had a sudden terrifying realization. She had lost it.

"I . . . didn't sleep very much last night," she said. "Maybe it's affecting my brain."

She fetched the pencil and sat down again, horribly aware of how closely Brody was watching her. The little room felt airless and uncomfortable.

"Tell me what's going on."

Brody's voice was gentle. Rhi tightened her grip on her pencil and stared fiercely at the page again.

"Rhi, I've been singing with you for long enough now to know when something is seriously bothering you. Is it about your parents? I know things aren't great at home right now." He hesitated. "The song we were working on yesterday. . ."

Rhi opened her mouth. She had no idea what was going to come out.

"My sister. . ." she began. "When she . . . when the accident happened, it broke us. We were never particularly great as a family, but Ruth . . . held us together. Now she's gone. And Dad's gone – he moved out yesterday. And Mum's not really there at all, except when she's shouting at me."

Somehow she was on her feet, tears running down her cheeks. Brody was holding her. She couldn't seem to stop talking now she'd started.

"It happened two years ago. She was killed in a car accident, there was a drunk driver. . . Everything in my life has gone so wrong, and I can't seem to change any of it," she sobbed against his shoulder. "When the police came and told us . . . it was the end of the world.

Mum might as well have been killed that day too, for all the life she has now. I can't go on being so unhappy. Help me, Brody."

"Shh," he said softly, rocking her in his arms. "You've had a tough time. It's OK to cry. It's okay to be sad."

Rhi cried until she her stomach hurt, and Brody's T-shirt was soaked through with her tears. Not once did he tell her to pull herself together.

"You . . . you won't leave me too, will you?" she croaked miserably, when at last the tears were gone.

He looked surprised. "Why would I do that? We're a team."

"But I can't write anything!"

"The music will come back."

Rhi wished she could feel so certain. "What if it doesn't?" she said desperately.

"Worrying about it isn't going to help. You have a natural songwriting ability, you know. You just have to let it flow."

Rhi stared up into Brody's crystal blue eyes. He really was amazing. There was no other word for him.

"You know everything, don't you?" she said in wonder.

A flush of colour stole into his cheeks. "Hardly. But I know that true talent doesn't just disappear."

His arms were warm around Rhi's back. She could have counted the faint freckles on his face, and the long eyelashes that framed his blue eyes. Being with him, having him hold her and understand her so clearly. . . Without thinking, Rhi moved her face towards his.

He let go of her so hurriedly that she almost fell over.

"You know you can talk to me any time, don't you?" he said. "Look, I'm sorry but I'm going to have to go. Something came up. I should have told you yesterday but I forgot. Remember what I said, OK? Let the music flow. You'll be fine."

Rhi was left staring at the swinging attic door once again. She had never felt so confused in her life.

NINE

Rhi wished she could stop thinking about Brody as she walked home, kicking listlessly at the stones that littered the pavement. He wasn't interested. She could feel herself blushing every time she remembered that horribly awkward moment when she thought he had been about to kiss her. What had *possessed* her to make a move like that?

The closer she got to home, the worse she felt. It was past midday, and she hadn't called her mother to say where she was, or what she was doing. She'd turned off her phone deliberately when she had left Lila's that morning. It had felt like a kind of escape. But no matter how slowly she walked, home was getting closer with every step.

At the door, Rhi took a deep breath. Setting her guitar down on the pavement, she slid her key into the door and turned.

Her mother was standing in the hallway.

"Good of you to turn up, Rhi," she said, resting her hands on her hips. "Where on earth have you been?"

Rhi didn't want to fight. She really didn't. "Sorry," she said quietly. "I left you a note in the kitchen about the sleepover at Lila's."

"Your friends should think more carefully about timing these sleepovers of theirs," her mother said with annoyance. "Have they forgotten you all have exams tomorrow?"

"We're hardly going to forget," said Rhi. She headed for the stairs.

"What about this morning?" said her mother, barring the way. "Don't tell me you only just woke up, Rhi. It's almost one o'clock in the afternoon. That's at least three hours' study time you've wasted!"

"I was writing songs with Brody," Rhi said evenly. "I do it every weekend, Mum, you know that."

"Songwriting with that boy," snorted her mother. "There's no future in these dreams of yours, Rhi. Honestly, you get more like your father every day."

Despite her best efforts to remain calm, Rhi could feel herself getting angry. "My singing isn't just a dream, Mum. It's what I want to do! Can't you for once just be happy for me?"

"I forbid you from seeing that boy until your exams are over," said her mother furiously.

What?

"Mum, we have gigs!" Rhi protested in horror. "They're booked and everything. There's no way I'm letting Brody down now!"

"So you're happy letting me down instead, are you?" her mother demanded. "Happy letting *yourself* down in this way?"

Rhi had to resist the urge to argue back. She winced as she remembered how horrible she'd been to her mother the day before. She didn't want it to happen again.

"You have always taught me about responsibility, Mum," she said in her calmest voice. "These gigs are my responsibility. People are counting on me to turn up and sing. I'm not letting Brody down."

Her mother muttered under her breath, and passed her hands through her hair. "Fine," she snapped, "you can do your gigs if you must. But there is to be no more all-day rehearsing at the weekends, do you hear me?"

"We never rehearse all day," said Rhi, unable to stop herself from sounding sullen.

"Don't use that tone with me, young lady. I don't like your attitude. If you fail these exams, a full ban might be in order. Do you understand me?"

Rhi couldn't believe how unreasonable her mother was being. A full ban if she failed her exams? No seeing Brody at all? "You're punishing me for what I said yesterday, aren't you?" she blurted.

"That's a ridiculous thing to say," her mother said at once. "I'm doing this because I care about your future, Rhi. Women need *careers*. They must be able to support themselves. I may be getting divorced, but at least I can take care of myself and don't have to rely on a man to do it for me. I don't want you to ruin your life over a boy, like I did with your father."

Rhi bit her lip so hard she could taste blood. "Have you finished?" she said stiffly.

"For now. I take it you haven't had lunch? Go and

make yourself a sandwich; there's some bread and ham in the kitchen. Then I want you to go upstairs and revise until I call you down for tea. Are we clear?"

Rhi stormed up the stairs, blood boiling through her veins. Slamming her bedroom door had never felt so satisfying. She glared at the notes still lying on her floor. Then she threw herself on the bed and screamed into her pillow. Rolling over, she stared in exhaustion at the ceiling. There was no way she would get any studying done feeling like this.

She pulled her phone from her pocket. Polly's name came up first. She waited for six rings before hanging up. Her heart was still racing with anger in her chest. Why did her mother have to be so awful?

Eve and Lila weren't picking up either. Rhi suddenly remembered the girls telling her that they all had plans with their significant others on Sunday afternoon. She dropped her phone on her bedside table with a groan, leapt to her feet and started pacing the room. She felt feverish and trapped, like a tiger in a cage.

Her foot brushed against something on the carpet. Rhi bent down and snatched up the crumpled ball of paper. She flattened it out and stared angrily at the words.

I'm sorry about everything. . . All I want is forgiveness. . .

This has to stop, she thought.

Mac had included his email address at the bottom of the letter. She flipped open her laptop and pulled up her email. She had to make him go away.

Don't contact me again, Mac. It's too painful.
Leave me alone.
Rhi

When she had sent it, Rhi rubbed her eyes and looked at Mac's pitiful letter again. Maybe she would forgive him one day, but not today. She was still too angry for forgiveness.

She had barely stood up from her desk when a reply landed in her inbox. She stared at it in surprise. She hadn't expected such a prompt response. Cautiously, she opened it.

I can't do that. I miss her. And I know you miss
her too.

Rhi's eyes blurred with tears for what felt like the hundredth time today. Why was Mac doing this to her? Didn't he know how much she was hurting? She wiped the tears angrily from her cheeks and, despite herself, read the rest of the message.

Someday I'd like to tell you what *really*
happened. I hope you'll let me do that.
Mac

Rhi stared at the words in confusion. They didn't make sense. What did Mac mean by "really happened"? Was there something about Ruth's death that she didn't know?

She slammed her laptop shut and rested her head on her desk. If Mac had wanted to pique her curiosity, he had succeeded. She hated him for it. Why had she emailed him at all?

The harder she tried not to think about Ruth, the more memories of her sister came pouring into her mind. Messing around at bathtime. Swingball in the garden. Holidays by the sea. Rhi couldn't prevent the images swirling through her mind. Ruth, smiling that maddening smile of hers, laughing and teasing and challenging.

"*Don't swing too high!*"

"*I'll swing as high as I like.*"

"*Mum will get mad!*"

"*I don't care. I'm flying, Rhi. Fly with me.*"

Rhi could feel a smile creeping across her face as she remembered Ruth flying on that swing. It felt strange to smile, but nice too.

She picked up her guitar and brushed the strings with her fingers. She needed to channel this emotion that she was feeling because it was the first good feeling she'd had in a while. There was no guilt, no terrible sadness. Hesitantly, she plucked out a little tune, hoping that it wouldn't vanish into thin air like her morning's attempt at music-making.

"Fly with me," she began. "To the blue air beyond . . . I'm not far, I'm so near, I can see you so clear; you are safe, you are free, fly with me. . ."

Her fingers steadied on the strings as the music

coursed through her. It felt as if Ruth was with her, encouraging her. Making her feel safe, just as the words and the music made her feel safe. She grabbed a pencil, scrawling the lyrics on the first piece of paper she could reach. *Fly with me.* . . She wanted to fly, she wanted it so badly. . . Ruth wouldn't let her fall.

"Stay with me, in a world full of light . . . keep the darkness at bay and take flight, I'm not far, I'm so near, I can see you so clear, as I hold out my arms, just to keep you from harm as you fly . . . fly with me. . ."

She rested her forehead on the neck of her guitar as the last chords died away. She felt better, as if Ruth was there with her again.

TEN

Rhi sat very still and watched the clock on the wall as it ticked endlessly towards midday. Heads were bent over desks all around her, the sound of scribbling pens filling the classroom. She stared at the page and a half of writing that she had put down on the paper in front of her. It wasn't enough. Her mother was right: she hadn't studied properly.

I don't need to wait for the result, she thought. *I know I've failed.* But she couldn't seem to make herself care.

After the exam, Rhi stayed quiet as her friends gathered in a relieved circle outside the hall.

"That was a shocker," Lila declared. "Even with all the work I put in with Josh, there's no way I've passed that."

Eve smirked. "Something tells me there was more kissing than revision with you two," she said.

"We did revise," Lila insisted, half laughing. "But OK – there was kissing too."

"Don't be so hard on yourself," said Polly encouragingly. "You probably did better than you think."

"I can't believe it's only Monday," Eve sighed. "We have four more days of this."

"Anyone want to come back to mine for a study session?" Polly offered. "Mum's back late tonight so we'll have the house to ourselves. I always revise better in company. Everyone has their notes for tomorrow's exams, right?"

It wasn't far to Polly's. Feeling relieved that she wouldn't have to go home yet, Rhi was happy to let Lila drag her out into the sunshine, and let the others chatter as she walked beside them. She wasn't in the mood for conversation.

"You're very quiet," Lila remarked as they turned into Polly's road. "Did your exam go OK?"

"I guess," Rhi found herself saying.

Lila squeezed her arm. "You'll be fine – you

always work really hard. What have you got tomorrow?"

Rhi wasn't sure she knew. What was wrong with her? Why couldn't she make herself care? "French and geography, I think," she said.

Lila looked admiring. "I wish I was as cool about these exams as you. I have my timetable practically tattooed on my eyelids."

Polly's house was bright and sunny, the kitchen table big enough for the four of them to fit around comfortably with a plate of biscuits and four mismatched mugs of tea. It was so calm here, Rhi reflected, looking around at the bright paintings on the walls and the well-thumbed books on the shelves. Her own house felt like a war zone in comparison.

She took out her books and wondered where to start.

Lila groaned. "I hate French."

"*Je déteste le français*," Eve observed.

Lila looked a little panic-stricken. "What?"

"I hate French," Eve replied.

Brightening, Lila said, "You too?"

"Eve said 'I hate French' in French, Lila," Rhi said, rousing herself. "She didn't actually mean she hated it."

Lila threw her hands in the air. "See what I'm up against?" she said in despair. "How am I supposed to do an exam in this? It's a foreign language."

"That's the point, I believe," said Eve drily.

Rhi opened a book at random and stared at it. If she could just focus, maybe she could absorb the information. But her mind was too full of other things.

"Rhi, can I talk to you?"

Rhi glanced up at Polly, twirling her pencil absently between her fingers. The others had their heads down over their books. "Sure. What about?"

"Let's go outside," Polly suggested.

Polly's garden was as bright and sunny as her kitchen, dotted with terracotta pots full of brightly coloured geraniums and daisies. Rhi felt the sun on her face as she sat down at the green garden table.

"What do you want to talk about?" she asked as Polly sat opposite her.

"I know what you're going through," said Polly simply. "It will get better, Rhi. I promise it will. Mum and Dad used to yell at each other outside in our garden. They thought if they shut the kitchen door, somehow I wouldn't be able to hear them."

Rhi gave a hollow laugh. "I wish my parents were as considerate."

"Have you seen your dad since he moved out?"

"I see him at the Heartbeat."

Rhi wasn't sure she wanted to talk about the Heartbeat all that much. It brought back the hot and miserable memory of her trying to kiss Brody and being rejected.

Polly's eyes glimmered with sympathetic tears. "Oh Rhi, I know this is awful. Any time you want to escape, you can come here, OK? It's really important to have a space where you can just *be*. I wish I'd had a space like that when I was going through it."

Rhi felt a wash of relief at the thought. "Thanks," she said gratefully. "I might take you up on that."

Polly reached over the table and gripped Rhi by the hands. "You know it might get worse before it gets better. Divorce isn't simple, or straightforward. I wish it was. It'll get interesting when one of them starts dating too."

"I thought you were trying to cheer me up!" Rhi said, with half a smile.

Polly looked anxious. "I am! The point I'm trying to make is that however bad it gets, it's important to remember that all the bad stuff will eventually pass and everything will get back to normal. It may be a different sort of normal, but it *will* be normal."

Rhi nodded. "It's been coming for a while, if I'm honest," she said. "They've been miserable for a long time. Dad told me he was thinking of leaving even before Ruth died." She blinked back a sudden rush of tears that had formed in the backs of her eyes. "My parents seem to bring out the worst in each other," she said sadly.

Polly nodded. "Mine did too."

Rhi wished more than anything that she could have her family back again, when everyone was happy, when Ruth was alive and there was nothing to worry about. *Talk about wishing for the stars*, she thought. "There *were* good times," she said, more to reassure herself than anything.

Polly smiled. "We had some really fun times when I was little. I like remembering us all around the kitchen table we had in our San Francisco apartment. The sun always seemed to shine. Dad used to make muffins. He was so proud of them, he made them at least once a week. They were always as hard as rocks but Mum and I pretended they were delicious." She giggled. "We fed most of them to the pigeons that used to land on our window sill. They were the fattest pigeons on the block."

"Mum and Dad used to have a water fights in the garden," Rhi said, remembering. "They were like a couple of kids."

"The key is to remember those good times without wishing you could have them back," Polly said.

Rhi swallowed painfully. "I don't think I can do that yet," she admitted.

Polly's voice was gentle. "Of course you can't, this has only just hit you. But you will be able to one day. I promise. You'll find your new normal, just like I have."

Rhi realized she was feeling better. "Yes," she said, feeling more confident. "You're right. It's just . . . getting to the new normal, isn't it?"

"Exactly. You'll all mess up for a while, and hurt each other, and shout and scream for a bit, and it'll suck," said Polly. She smiled encouragingly. "But then things will settle down and a kind of calm will sneak up on you that you won't even notice for a while. And then – bang. New normal."

ELEVEN

Finding herself unable to concentrate, Rhi left Polly's house earlier than the others, intending to go home. Instead, she found herself down on the beach, curled up among the rocks where she had sat only a few days earlier, watching the sea and thinking. It wasn't until the tide began to lap at her toes that she stood up and started the long trudge home. Her school bag felt absurdly heavy on her back.

It started the moment she came through the door.

"How was your first exam?" Her mother's eyes flicked over Rhi's sandy uniform. "It's late. Where have you been?"

Rhi paused on the stairs. At least she could look her

mother in the eye on this one. "Studying at Polly's with the others."

Her mother looked relieved. "Thank goodness you're starting to take things more seriously. I hope you were working and not chattering?"

The quiet haven of her bedroom was so close. "Not now, Mum," Rhi said, reaching for her door handle.

Her mother was up the stairs in a flash, standing beside Rhi as she tried to get into her room. "What does that mean? You *were* studying, weren't you?"

Rhi went into her room and shut the door as firmly as she dared. All she wanted to do was pick up her guitar and work on the song she'd written for Ruth the day before. She'd been thinking about it down on the beach, and she knew it wasn't quite as she wanted it. The rhymes were still rough around the edges, and the chorus wasn't right. She put down her bag and slung her guitar around her neck, closed her eyes and summoned up the opening chords of the song.

The door opened. Rhi swung round. Her mother folded her arms and raised her eyebrows enquiringly at the guitar around Rhi's neck.

"I didn't say you could come in!" Rhi blurted.

Her mother made an inarticulate sound of frustration. "How many times do I have to tell you, you don't have time for singing songs right now! You have two exams tomorrow, French and geography. . ."

"You think I don't know that?" Rhi shouted.

"Don't shout at me, Rhi. I've had a difficult day. I don't know what else to say to you that will make you realize—"

"Leave me alone, Mum!" Rhi yelled. "Just . . . *go away*!"

"I've done what I can," her mother said stiffly, heading out to the landing again. "Your results will prove me right, young lady. Just mark my word. It's your life."

Only it wasn't, it seemed to Rhi. Everywhere she turned, her mother was there, hanging watchfully over her shoulder, trying to steer her into her own idea of what Rhi's life should be. It was starting to drive Rhi mad.

On Tuesday, French passed in a haze of half-finished sentences and blank spaces. There wasn't even a question on irrigation in East Anglia in the geography paper in the afternoon. Rhi dragged herself home straight after school, endured her mother's questions, and barricaded herself in her room. She even wedged a chair under the door handle to prevent any unannounced visits, although the chair didn't prevent her mother from knocking and saying in acid tones through the door: "I'm sure you'd pass a guitar exam with flying colours, Rhi. I wish I had the same confidence in the exams that actually *matter*."

Wednesday was the easiest day of the week, with only an art exam and a French oral to cope with. The sea air had never smelled so sweet as Rhi hurried out of school with her guitar bouncing on her back. Wednesday night was Heartbeat Café night. A chance to play and sing. An opportunity to see her dad and talk to him. And precious time with Brody. She deserved all three after the week she'd been through.

Her dad was behind the counter, sorting out the big coffee machine. "Rhi!" he exclaimed, setting down various parts of chrome machinery and hurrying out to greet her. "How is exam week going?"

"It just got a lot better," Rhi said happily, letting him fold her into his arms.

The café was looking a little different from usual. The tables and chairs had been pushed aside and easels dotted the room. Rhi counted ten people clustered around the easels with palettes and brushes in their hands, staring at a still-life arrangement of fruit, plates and glasses that had been set up in front of the stage. The smell of paint in the air was strong.

"Afternoon workshop," said her dad, noticing Rhi's gaze. "It's all kicking off in here. Ever since that wedding show you and Eve helped me put together the other day, I've been full to bursting with bookings. Art exhibitions, fashion events, that kind of thing. Wedding receptions too. There's one here on Saturday."

"I know," Rhi said. "Brody and I are singing."

Her father nodded. "Of course you are, I'd forgotten. Anyway, through my contacts at the gallery, I've started an art class, as you can see. It was supposed to be mornings only, but the demand was there for an afternoon workshop as well."

"You look happy," Rhi said, smiling up at him. She was so glad to see him.

"I am," he admitted. He looked at his painting class with pride. "Some of them are actually quite good. Listen love, can you help me with the coffee machine? Some of my students are struggling."

Rhi took over behind the counter as her dad hurried over to his pupils, helping them to hold their paintbrushes more effectively and mix the right colours on their palettes. The whole class was made up of women, she realized. She wasn't sure she liked the way some of them were looking at her father. Like they were flirting. Several of them had piercing laughs that they used a bit too often. The sound set Rhi's teeth on edge, but her dad seemed to be enjoying the attention.

He'll soon be single, she reminded herself, biting her lip. It was the weirdest thought. She couldn't imagine her dad out with anyone other than her mother.

Polly had warned her that things might get weird when her parents started dating other people. She hadn't said anything about the dating thing happening right away.

He and Mum have only just split up, she thought in dismay.

The coffee machine was like a giant chrome jigsaw puzzle. However hard Rhi tried to concentrate on putting it back together the way her father had shown her, her eyes kept darting back to her dad and the women. One woman in particular seemed to be getting very touchy-feely. Every time her father passed by, she would reach out and touch him on the elbow, drawing him down to her for a murmured conversation.

"Dad," Rhi blurted across the counter. "Can I ask you something? It's really important."

Her father excused himself from his pupils. "What is it?"

Rhi smiled at him hopefully. "Can I see your flat?"

He looked surprised. "Of course, if you'd like to. It's just down the street from here. Ladies, can you wrap this up by yourselves? See you same time next week." He held up a hand to his class, who all waved their paintbrushes back.

Her father's new home was a three-storey climb from the street, and Rhi found herself a little out of breath as he pulled out a set of keys.

"Home sweet home," he said, pushing the door open.

The flat *was* sweet, with low ceilings and an open-plan layout. Paintings were stacked against the white plastered walls, and stacks of paint supplies and sketchbooks cluttered every available surface. There was a large bedroom and a small box room, with a view over the town roofs and just enough space for a desk and a bed. In the main living space, two small windows looked out towards the sea. Her dad had set up an easel in the sunniest spot in the room, where light poured into the small space from a skylight.

There was what looked like a half-finished painting of a woman on the easel. Before Rhi could get a proper look at it, her dad hastily covered it with an oily bit of tarpaulin.

"What do you think?" he said, spreading his hands.

"It's bigger than I was expecting." Rhi gazed curiously at the covered easel one more time, then walked over to the pile of paintings stacked against the walls. She picked up the first one: a still life of pebbles and driftwood. Around the edge of the image, her father had captured the foamy frill of seawater as it swept towards the pebbles.

"This is really good, Dad," Rhi said, staring at the image.

"Do you think so? It was really hard to do that one. The pebbles kept drying out when I was trying to capture their colours. But I'm pleased with the end result." He smiled with pride. "I'm painting so much at the moment, you wouldn't recognize me."

He looked happier than Rhi could ever remember. Life in this place suited him. She set the pebble picture aside and picked up another one of a beady-eyed gull on a barnacled rock. Its expression was almost comical.

"You're an amazing artist, Dad," she said in wonder. "Why don't we have more of your paintings at home?"

"Your mother was never very keen," he said wryly.

Rhi had a flash vision of going back home tonight, having to face more questions and arguments from her mother. She closed her eyes, hoping to somehow ward off the image.

"Can I come and live with you?" she said, opening her eyes again. "I could have the box room."

Her father looked anxious. "Rhi, we've talked about this. There isn't room and you need peace for your exams—"

"Peace?" Rhi echoed incredulously. "There's no peace around Mum. You should know that better than anyone. *Please* can I move in? I don't need much space, honestly I don't." Her eyes darted around the little room, settling on a long red sofa against one wall. "Polly has said I can study round at her house. I can't go back home. I don't want to live there. I want to live with you, and look after you."

Rhi's father started pacing restlessly from side to side. "It's impossible, Rhi. I keep strange hours, up all night painting . . . I can't have anyone else here. It's not the right place for you. You really are better off with your mother."

He was keeping something from her. The way he wouldn't meet her eye – she knew that look. Rhi could feel her heart breaking into pieces.

"You don't care about me at all," she whispered.

"Of course I care! This . . . it's difficult to explain. . . Rhi darling, please don't cry. . . Come back!"

What was he not telling her? Why was the woman in the picture so hurriedly covered up? Everyone was keeping secrets, Rhi thought as she rushed away down the stairs. First Brody and his song, and now her dad. She couldn't bear it.

Who are you to judge? said the little voice in her mind. *You're keeping the biggest secret of all.*

TWELVE

By the time Rhi came back into the Heartbeat Café, the art group had gone, taking their pictures, paint and easels with them. All that remained was the still life in the centre of the room. It had a surreal quality to it now that the class had gone.

Good riddance, Rhi thought with a sudden rush of fury. The only reason the women came was to flirt with her father. She thought of the half-finished picture of the woman on the easel her father had covered up. For a moment, she felt as if she was going to be sick.

Brody appeared from the stage door, his guitar around his neck. "Hey," he said. He gestured at the still life. "What do you think your dad wants us to do with this?"

Rhi couldn't even summon the strength to smile. "Don't ask me. I didn't even know he had an art class." There was a lot she didn't know about her dad at the moment.

Brody contemplated it. "Maybe we should eat it," he said. "We could use the plates."

The fruit did look kind of tempting. Rhi imagined the class rolling up and gaping at a bowl of orange skin, banana peel and mouldy apple cores. When Brody grinned at her, she felt her heart lightening. He had the loveliest smile.

"Give me a hug," he said.

Rhi went gladly into his arms. She fitted against him so well. Sometimes it felt like she never needed to be anywhere else, ever again.

"I'm sorry for running off again on Sunday," he said over her head.

Rhi tried not to remember how embarrassed she had felt. "You needed to be somewhere else," she said against his T-shirt, snuggling a little closer to him. "It wasn't a problem, honestly."

When she felt him tense under her fingers, she stepped away quickly, keen to avoid giving him the wrong impression all over again. When would she learn that he didn't want things to go any further?

"So." Brody slid his hands into his back pockets, and then into his front pockets, like he wasn't sure where to put them. "What are we singing tonight?"

Think about the music, Rhi told herself. "I want to try a new song," she said bravely. "After that weird mental block I had on Sunday, I did as you said and tried to let the music flow. I've got something that I really hope you'll like."

"Great! Don't play it to me now – save it." He pushed a stray curl out of Rhi's eyes and smiled. "You can blow me away along with the rest of the crowd. I know it'll be brilliant because *you* are."

Rhi wanted to kiss him so badly she could hardly breathe. "Thanks," she said, swallowing. "You know – for your faith in me. I hope I won't let you down."

They stared at each other. *This should be so easy*, Rhi thought hopelessly. *The way he looks at me. . .*

Brody broke eye contact. "I guess we should move the still life backstage," he said, looking back at the bowl of fruit with its glasses and plates. "Give me a hand?"

And just like that, the moment was gone.

By the time they returned from stowing the still-life table, Rhi's father was behind the bar, wiping glasses. Before Rhi could speak to him, the doors banged open and her friends streamed inside.

"I hope you've got some good tunes tonight, guys." As usual, Ollie's arm was draped around Polly's shoulders. "I need something to take my mind off my terrible German oral this afternoon. It was about health and I totally forgot the words for hospital and doctor. I just kept saying 'hospital' and 'doctor' in my best German accent and hoped for the best."

"German is such an ugly language," said Eve with a shudder. "French is so much better. Chanel, Givenchy, Dior. . ."

"Karl Lagerfeld is German," Polly said. 'You know, the Chanel designer."

"I know who Karl Lagerfeld is, Polly," said Eve. "I saw him once in Paris." For a moment, Eve looked wistful.

"What's everyone got tomorrow?" asked Ollie, looking anxious.

"More art," said Josh happily. "My favourite."

"Urgh," said Lila, unwrapping herself from Josh for long enough to press her hands to her ears. "We haven't come out to talk about exams, have we? I thought we were here for a good time."

"And some good music," Polly added, smiling at Rhi.

The café was filling up already. Wednesdays at the Heartbeat had developed a reputation, and the place was usually full. Rhi felt a flutter of nerves as she settled down at the table with her friends, aware of the way people looked at her now – like she was a little bit famous. She and Brody would be singing in an hour, and she would showcase her new song. A mixture of excitement and terror swirled in her belly at the thought. She had been singing her song about Ruth a lot this week, locked away in her room, playing softly so her mother wouldn't hear. The words and the tune brought her sister back to life in a way Rhi had never dared to hope for.

"Ready?"

Rhi took the hand Brody was holding out to her, trying to ignore the loaded glances of her friends, and followed him backstage. She was determined to sing well tonight, and do Ruth proud.

The room went crazy for "Fast Lane Freak" as

usual. The song had become a Wednesday night tradition, but somehow it never got stale. They sang several of the covers they'd done at the hippy wedding, and a new one they'd been working on for a couple of weeks called "Seagull Blues".

"The last song tonight is a surprise," said Brody into the microphone when their set finally drew to a close. "At least, it's a surprise to me. But not to Rhi. Hopefully."

Several people laughed.

"They're all yours," said Brody, turning to Rhi with an encouraging smile. "Knock 'em out."

Rhi hoped she wasn't going to mess this up. She tuned her guitar and closed her eyes, summoning Ruth to her side as she leaned into the mic.

"This is a song called "With You By Myself". I wrote it for my sister. Ruth died two years ago now, but she's right here in the song. At least, she is to me. I hope she is to you too."

Rhi glanced at the bar. Her father looked as if he had been turned to stone.

"Fly with me," she began bravely. "To the blue air beyond. . ."

She'd spent a long time this week refining the rhyme and rhythm of the song, playing long and soft into the night, hoping her mother wouldn't hear the strumming guitar. *Are you listening, Ruth? Can you hear how I loved you?*

"Stay with me, in a world full of light . . . keep the darkness at bay and take flight. . ."

It was working, Rhi realized exultantly. Ruth was there, beside her on the stage. A flash of colour at the corner of her eye, an echo of laughter. She lifted her voice as the song surged onwards.

"I thought I would fail, I thought I would fall – but flying alone isn't lonesome at all, because you aren't far, you're so very near, you're deep in my heart and you won't disappear, I'm flying with you but I'm all by myself . . . I'm flying with you but I'm all by myself."

The silence that followed the last chord seemed endless. Then, in a blink, the whole room was cheering and stomping and calling Rhi's name. Feeling a little overwhelmed, she glanced at Brody for reassurance.

Brody's eyes seemed to be shining with their own blue fire. He grabbed her and held her close, rocking with her right there on the stage. "Amazing doesn't begin to describe that song," he said into her ear as the cheering in the room grew louder. "Your sister would be so, so proud."

"Thank you," Rhi whispered.

As she pulled back from Brody's embrace, waving and smiling tearfully at the appreciative crowd, her eye snagged on a hat near the back of the room.

In a flash she knew it was the boy in the wheelchair from the pensioners' wedding. She half-lifted her hand to wave, before realizing how stupid she would look. She hadn't even met the guy. It looked like she had a mystery fan.

"Thank you. . . Thank you so much. . ."

Rhi wanted to find the boy and talk to him, ask him why he had left the wedding and why he was here. As the applause finally died away, she propped her guitar against her stool, jumped off the stage, and strode towards the back of the room. Why was it so important? She didn't know. Her feet seemed to be moving of their own accord.

"That was great. Really moving," someone offered as she strode past. "I cried and I never cry."

Over the tops of the crowd Rhi could see the doors

of the café swinging gently on their hinges. Determined not to lose him this time, she hurried through the doors – and stopped, staring in frustration at the empty street.

There was no one in the alley leading to the Heartbeat Café's back doors. No one in the cobbled cut-through to the beach. The steep steps leading up to the High Street would be impossible for a wheelchair. Rhi wanted to scream. She'd lost him again.

My friends must think I'm mad, she thought, heading back towards the café in defeat. It looked like her mystery fan would have to remain a mystery.

As she reached for the café's door handles, she glimpsed the heel of Brody's red Converse disappearing up the steps to the High Street. He hadn't said he was going anywhere after the gig, had he? She'd have remembered.

Rhi'd had enough secrets to last a lifetime. She had to know where Brody was going. So she turned away from the Heartbeat's wooden doors, and followed him at a safe distance.

THIRTEEN

Rhi headed up the cobbled steps, determined to see where Brody was going at this time of the evening. Why hadn't he said anything? He'd been running off a lot recently, now she thought about it. All those occasions when he'd called a halt to their rehearsing and dashed away. There was always "somewhere he had to be". What if he had a girlfriend he hadn't told Rhi about? Rhi felt cold at the thought as she turned into the High Street at the top of the steps. If he had a girlfriend he was keeping secret, what else hadn't he told her?

How much did she really know about Brody?

Rhi couldn't think of a single personal conversation that they'd had that hadn't revolved around her. She blushed at the thought. She had been so self-centred that she'd never asked him *anything* about himself.

What kind of a friend didn't ask a person a single question about their lives? She knew everything about Lila, Eve and Polly, but precisely zero about the boy she had been dreaming about for weeks.

How was that even possible?

The air was growing colder as Rhi sneaked from doorway to doorway. When she felt the first splash of cold rain on the back of her neck, she almost leaped out of her skin. She'd left in such a hurry, and hadn't picked up her jacket. She was going to get drenched. Maybe she should just return to the warm, dry café with her friends and forget this madness.

Keeping Brody firmly in her sights, she pressed on.

The town looked different in the rain. Darker, quieter. The only sound was the occasional car swishing past and the drum of rain on the rooftops and the pavements. Rhi had reached the stage where she was so wet that her shoes squelched and her hair hung limply around her face. If her reflection in the shop windows was anything to go by, she looked like a freak, but she didn't care. All she cared about was not losing sight of Brody.

Brody moved quickly along the road, his blond hair darkened by the rain. His guitar case was zipped firmly against the weather, his collar turned up to protect him from the downpour. He was going somewhere he'd been to before, that much was clear. There were no hesitations at road junctions, no checking directions on his phone. Was he going home? Rhi could feel herself blushing even more deeply as she realized she didn't even know where Brody lived.

It was insane that she had shared so much of her soul with someone so mysterious to her. The more she thought about it, the more she understood that Brody had only done his sharing through their music.

They were climbing the hill now. A bus flew past, and Rhi jumped back automatically at the spray of water thrown up by its wheels. She almost felt like laughing. Even if the bus had splashed her, she couldn't have got any wetter.

As she looked round for Brody again, she panicked. She'd lost him. She was useless at tracking people. Had she got this wet and come all this way, just to lose Brody as she had lost the boy in the wheelchair?

Squinting from beneath the bus shelter, she finally

spotted a Brody-shaped figure heading towards an old church on the corner. Her heart rate steadied again. All was not lost after all. But . . . a *church*? Was Brody religious? Rhi couldn't imagine it. But what did she know?

She hesitated outside the church gate. Maybe she should leave Brody alone. This felt private. Then again, if she didn't follow him inside, she might never know why he'd gone in there. Suddenly it felt like the most important thing in the world to know.

St Saviour's was Heartside Bay's oldest church. Rhi had passed it hundreds of times, but had never set foot inside. It was popular for many of the weddings that took place in Heartside Bay as it was incredibly picturesque with a meadow-like churchyard and a neat little lychgate leading off the street. At this time of night it was hard to picture it full of chattering guests in brightly coloured hats, its winding flagstone path covered in pastel-coloured confetti. Right now it didn't feel romantic at all; just dark and a little forbidding, particularly with the rain darkening its great stone walls.

Rhi heard the boom of the closing church door as

Brody went inside. Still not convinced she was doing the right thing, she squeezed through the gate and tried not to slip on the rain-slicked flagstones leading to the main door. She opened the big wooden door and peered nervously inside.

There was no one there. Candles flickered on the altar, and in several small side chapels. A smell of old stones and incense hung in the air.

Water was beginning to puddle around Rhi's feet. She shivered, rubbing her arms. It was warmer outside. Brody was in here somewhere – she had *seen* him come inside. The silence was unnerving her. She scanned the big cork noticeboard in the porch a little hopelessly, wondering what to do next.

AA MEETING TODAY

NEWMAN ROOM

TAKE THE STAIRS IN THE SACRISTY

ALL WELCOME!

The words were printed in bold on a yellow background, the letters "AA" inside a triangle with the words Unity, Service, and Recovery written along the three sides. Rhi stared at the poster with a creeping sense of unease. AA? As in . . . Alcoholics Anonymous?

Before she could talk herself out of it, she walked towards the back of the church and took a flight of stone steps that curved down to a lighted basement. It was more modern down here than she had expected: a little kitchen, a toilet – and a plain wooden door with a glass panel at eye level. She paused at the door and stared through the little panel into the room beyond.

Eight people were sitting in a circle. A ninth stood at a podium directly facing the door. Looking right at her.

Rhi gasped and stumbled back from the door the moment she met Brody's eyes. It couldn't be true.

"Rhi!" Brody yelled, jumping down from the podium. The others turned and stared curiously towards the panel in the door.

I can't be here, Rhi thought in horror.

Whirling around, she raced back up the stone steps and into the church again, her wet feet slapping against the stones and leaving footprints. She sprinted through the porch, barged against the wooden doors with her shoulder, and fled back out into the evening, intent on leaving Brody behind her. She couldn't speak to him. . .

The rain was still pelting down but Rhi raced on heedless, slipping and sliding on the flagstone path, flying through the gate and skidding away down the road. Her shocked brain was moving almost faster than her legs. In her mind's eye, she heard the squeal of brakes, the swerve of wheels, the hideous scrunch of metal. She pictured Ruth's eyes widening in horror, then closing for ever. A drunk driver. *A drunk driver*. . .

Brody was an alcoholic, like the person who had killed her sister.

FOURTEEN

It can't be true. It can't be. . .

Of all the secrets Rhi might have imagined, this was the worst. She'd had no idea. Brody. . . The driver of the car that had killed her sister. . . Drunk. Drunk. *Drunk. . .*

Snakes in her head, coiling and writhing. Rhi ran faster but still they hissed, their black tongues flickering and their fangs extended, poised to strike. Halfway down the road she stumbled over the kerb and went sprawling to the ground. The physical pain of the bloodied scrape on her knees was a relief as, for a moment, it distracted her from her thoughts.

But she couldn't let Brody catch her.

Picking herself up, she pelted up an alleyway, down

a fenced path, past a jumble of warehouses. She was heading downhill, she knew that much. The snakes knew it too.

How could she have been so blind?

The beach. The sea. Rhi ran on, her feet pounding on the packed wet sand. When she reached the water's edge she stopped, gasping for air, pressing her hands to her aching sides. Blood trailed down her legs, mingling with the damp salt air. The wounds stung.

He was behind her, gasping almost as much as she was. She had no need to turn round to confirm it. She hadn't run far enough.

"Rhi, please! Let me explain!"

Rhi gazed numbly out to sea. "There's nothing to explain," she said. She could feel her teeth chattering together as the cold rain seemed to soak into her bones. "I shouldn't have followed you. I wish I hadn't. I'm sorry."

"Rhi, please look at me." He sounded desperate. "We need to talk about this."

Rhi turned slowly.

Brody was just as bedraggled as she was. He looked at her with eyes that were dark and full of pain.

"You're drenched," he began, reaching out a hand to touch her sleeve. "You're going to get sick. Let's talk about this somewhere that's out of the rain."

Rhi flinched away from him. She liked the feel of the rain washing over her. She wished it could wash all her problems away. "How could you not tell me something like this?" she said. Her voice shook despite her best efforts. "Brody, I thought we were close. I thought. . ." *I thought maybe you liked me.* She left her sentence unfinished. It seemed pointless now.

"I wanted to tell you so badly," he said, "but I could never find the right moment. 'Hey Rhi, how are you doing, love the song, by the way I'm an alcoholic' – it's kind of a buzzkill. I was scared of what you might say. How it would change the way you thought about me."

Raindrops were shimmering on his eyelashes. Or maybe they were tears. Rhi wondered how you could tell the difference.

"I'm so, so sorry for keeping the whole AA thing from you," he went on quietly. "I've kept it from everybody. It's not exactly something I'm proud of. I was going to tell you this weekend, but then you told me what happened to your sister and . . . I couldn't."

113

Rhi's feet felt like blocks of ice now. She pushed her sopping wet hair out of her face. "Are you still drinking?" she asked as steadily as she could.

He tipped his head back and gazed up into the rain, running his hands through his hair. Then he looked at her again and shook his head. "I've been sober for nearly a year. I swear it."

Did she believe him? Rhi didn't know. It was like the raindrops and the tears. How could you tell the difference between the truth and a lie?

"Please believe me, Rhi," he pleaded. "I couldn't bear it if this ruined things between us. You're too precious to me."

Rhi caught herself before she softened. Too much was at stake to mess this up.

"How often do you go to your meetings?"

"Whenever I can. But at least once a week." He looked older than she'd ever seen him. "Alcoholism is something that stays with you for life. You have to know that to have any hope of fighting it. Sometimes it's small things that set you off, and sometimes it's bigger than that. Problems, dramas. You want to reach for a drink to take the problem away. You go to a meeting and the need is easier to manage. You know you're not alone."

Rhi forced herself to ask the next question. "Did you ever drink and drive, Brody?"

"I did a lot of stupid, scary things when I was drunk," he admitted. "The truth is that I can't remember half of what I did, and that's the most terrifying thing of all. But it's in the past now. I swear it to you, on my life. On my guitar. On everything that matters to me." He paused. "I swear it on you."

A fresh wave of tears felt hot on Rhi's cheeks.

"Music has been my salvation." His voice was growing more urgent. "It's everything to me. It's how I cope, and it's how I make sense of my life. When I play, when I sing . . . somehow, I don't need to drink. Making music is all the comfort that I need. Especially when I make it with you."

He came closer to her, cupping her face in his ice-cold hands. Rhi didn't push him away. She found that she couldn't. She stared into his eyes as they blazed at her with the relief of a secret kept too long.

"My AA sponsor told me not to get involved in any new relationships for at least a year. But I can't help it, Rhi. I've tried, but there's nothing I can do. I'm completely and utterly in love with you."

His lips crushed against hers, hot and cold at the same time. Rhi instantly found herself kissing him back as if her life depended on it, her hands around his back and in his hair. Despite the chill of the rain still hammering down on their heads, she wasn't cold any more.

"You're so beautiful," he whispered against her mouth. "I've wanted this for so long. . ."

Rhi had wanted this too, more than anything. His kisses were so passionate they were making her dizzy. They were soulmates. She loved him. But. . .

This couldn't happen.

Did you ever drink and drive? Ruth watched her with expressionless eyes.

Rhi gave a sobbing gasp and pulled away from Brody's arms. She felt cold all over again, and more broken than ever.

"I can't do this," she said in despair. "I'm sorry. . ."

And she ran back up the beach with her head down and her heart scattered across the sand behind her.

FIFTEEN

Rhi had very little memory of her exams over the next few days.

It had turned out that she wasn't immune to the rain and cold after all. She shivered and sneezed her way through four hours on subjects she found that she had forgotten about almost as soon as she had laid her pen down and handed her paper in. She wrote blindly, seeing Brody's face with every sentence she scribbled. His blazing blue eyes, the feeling of his lips as he had kissed her. . . Her whole body boiled at the memory. It wasn't easy to bring her thoughts back to calculus, or *Hamlet*.

"Only two more to go," Polly said as they all trailed exhaustedly out of English literature on Thursday. "Study session at mine?"

"I'd prefer an ice-cream session at the Heartbeat," Lila groaned.

Rhi sucked throat sweets and blew her nose and hoped no one would start curious questions about where she'd gone after the previous night's gig. It was a vain hope.

Polly started first. "Where did you *go*, Rhi? You were so brilliant, especially that last song about Ruth. We'd ordered you a massive hot chocolate to celebrate and you vanished! Ollie had to drink it all by himself!"

"I suffered," said Ollie seriously.

"Brody left about the same time as you did," Josh observed. His arm, as ever, was around Lila's waist.

Eve's grey eyes were bright with curiosity. "Were you with Guitar Hero? Confess it all, Rhi."

"Brody and Rhi sitting in a tree," giggled Lila.

"S-I-N-G-I-N-G!" Rhi said, as firmly as she could, and left before anyone asked her anything else.

She couldn't bear to think about Brody just now. It was too painful. She had already deleted four despairing texts from him that morning. *We can make this work. Don't cut me out. Talk to me. Kiss me in the rain again.* She knew them all by heart, despite deleting them as soon as she had read them. It was taking all her willpower right now not to take her phone out of her bag and check for more.

Did she love him? She thought she did. Every time she remembered their kiss, she got goosebumps all over. They were attracted to each other, certainly. But could she honestly commit to Brody? She thought she'd known him, but her faith in him was based on thin air. She didn't know him at all. Maybe the guy she loved didn't even exist.

Her head ached every time she tried to answer that one.

Friday wasn't much better, although her throat had eased by lunchtime. She had hardly made it out of the examination hall that afternoon when she was almost bowled over by Ollie.

"WHOO!" he shouted, racing at full speed down the corridor. "SCHOOL'S OUT!"

"No running, Mr Wright," shouted Mr Morrison, their form teacher, putting his head out of the staffroom door a fraction too late.

"I'd like to see Mr Morrison try to stop him," Eve laughed. The corridor was full of relieved students hugging each other. "Summer's here, darlings. Can't you taste it?"

They could still hear Ollie whooping his way down the corridor.

"I'm am SO glad it's over," Lila squealed. "No more exams for months! I need to leave now and eat chocolate and listen to music and dance and have FUN. Are you coming, Josh?"

Josh slid his bag over his shoulder and smiled at Lila. "In a heartbeat."

The look in his eyes made Rhi's heart hurt. Brody had looked at her like that on Wednesday night, and she had pushed him away.

"In *the* Heartbeat you mean," Polly laughed. "Ollie's probably there already, he was moving so fast."

The sun was shining warmly on the steps of the school as they left. Everyone around her was chattering and laughing. Rhi tried to smile and look as pleased as everyone else, but she couldn't do it. Brody was bound to be at the Heartbeat. Whatever was she going to say to him?

The Heartbeat was already half-full of other people

celebrating when they got there. Rhi stayed at the back of the crowd as Josh pushed open the doors, holding them open with a bow.

Max was at their usual table, his arm around a girl Rhi recognized from Year Nine. He didn't even acknowledge them as they selected their second favourite table right beside the bar. Rhi felt nothing at all. Not a jolt, not a moment of regret. How could she have spent so long going out with a boy she hardly even thought about any more? It was a mystery.

"When is Max going to stop sulking about Rhi?" Eve asked, sliding along the padded bench to make room for the others. "He's got to move on."

"He already has, if the girl on his arm is anything to go by," Rhi observed.

The others glanced at each other.

"Are you OK with that?" Polly checked, laying her hand on Rhi's sleeve.

If there was one thing Rhi felt certain about in the mess that constituted her life, it was that she was over Max Holmes. "I'm fine," she said. "Really."

"She's got Guitar Hero to think about now," Eve

drawled, sipping on her frappe. "And I don't want to over-excite you, Rhi, but he's heading this way."

The smile froze on Rhi's face as she registered Brody in the door of the Heartbeat Café, looking gorgeous in a blue shirt that matched his eyes. He was looking right at her. She couldn't panic in front of her friends; it would be too embarrassing. Instead, she picked up her bag, got to her feet and walked towards him. Her legs felt like jelly.

"Hi," he said when she reached him.

Rhi tried to swallow her nerves and smile, horribly aware of her friends watching her every move. "Hi," she mumbled.

He looked at her. "Exams go OK?"

"Mm-hmm." *Full marks for conversational prowess*, she thought hopelessly.

"Good to hear it. Did you get my messages?"

She could hardly say no, could she? "It . . . they were lovely," Rhi managed to answer. She could feel herself blushing. "I'm sorry I didn't reply."

"There's still time," he said. His eyes were so blue. So pleading.

I can't do this, Rhi wanted to shout. "Sorry," she

said, backing towards the café door. She was terrified she might start crying. "I'm just . . . I can't be with you right now, Brody. I'll sing at tomorrow's wedding reception here with you but . . . I can't be here now. I have to go."

She bolted. Brody's stricken face stayed with her the whole way home.

Stupid, stupid, stupid. Rhi raged at herself as she walked furiously along her street. Why couldn't she get this together? This was *Brody*. Her singing partner. Her future – at least musically. How was she ever going to sing with him again, feeling the way she did? How had she messed things up so royally? She was already dreading the wedding reception at the Heartbeat the following day, but she'd made a commitment. She wouldn't break it. Even if it broke *her*.

As she wearily put her key in the door and turned the latch, a familiar sound greeted her. Her mother was shouting at her dad down the phone.

"Why did I even agree to talk to you, Patrick? You never change. You never listen to a word I say."

This is all I need, Rhi thought through gritted teeth.

She walked steadily towards the stairs. Her mother didn't seem to notice her at all.

"You don't seem to realize how ridiculous all of this is. . . You haven't got a shred of common sense. . . How I ever married you in the first place is beyond me—"

Rhi shut her bedroom door. It helped a little. She put her guitar carefully on her bed, trying not to think about the expression on Brody's face as she'd run away from him tonight. It was difficult.

To distract her, she picked up her favourite photo of her family and tried to lose herself in the memories. The four of them in Trafalgar Square, laughing as if they'd all just heard the funniest joke in the world. It felt a very long time ago.

Someday I'd like to tell you what really happened. . . Mac's cryptic email resurfaced in her mind. Had there been more to Ruth's death than she had realized? She flipped open her laptop and logged on. Then she pulled up Mac's email and stared at it. She needed a distraction from the rest of her life. Maybe this was it.

She started typing.

Mac

Meet me tomorrow at Ruth's grave? I'll be

there. 11am.

Rhi

SIXTEEN

"Go if you must," her mother sighed at Rhi at the breakfast table the next morning.

"I've had exams all week, Mum," Rhi pointed out. "I just need a break, OK?"

"If you'd worked a little harder for your exams, I might agree with you, Rhi," said her mother. "But they're in the past now and we'll just have to hope for the best. Whereabouts in London are you going?"

Rhi wasn't about to give her mother details.

"I don't know," she said, deliberately vague. "Somewhere central. Shopping, maybe."

"It seems that's all young people want to do these days." Her mother put the lid on the jam with more force than necessary. "Is this Lila's idea? I still think that girl is trouble."

It was an old argument that Rhi wasn't prepared to have right now. She discreetly checked her watch. She had half an hour to catch the train.

"Can I?" she persisted.

"I said you could go, didn't I?" Rhi's mother checked her own watch before snatching up her jacket and bag. "I need to be in the surgery in fifteen minutes. I'll try to have some dinner ready when you get home, but I can't guarantee it."

Her mother's idea of cooking was to throw some vegetables into a pot and stir vigorously for half an hour. The cooking had always been done by Rhi's dad, and Rhi's mother had never bothered to learn much beyond the basics. It was yet another thing that made Rhi mad. Her mother never acknowledged the things her dad did for their family.

The morning was blustery as Rhi walked down the hill towards the station. After stowing her guitar and outfit for that afternoon's wedding in a locker ready for her return, she stood on the platform, trying to blend in with the Saturday crowd. There seemed to be groups of people all travelling together, laughing and talking about their plans for the day. It felt strange to be standing here without her friends. Trying to look busy, she took out her phone and stared at it.

Mum would have a fit if she knew I was travelling by myself today, she thought. *Let alone if she knew who I was going to meet.*

Rhi could hardly believe it herself. Mac had replied almost as soon as she'd sent the email last night: *I'll be there*. Rhi hadn't slept well for worrying about how the meeting was going to turn out.

The train seemed to take for ever. Rhi checked her watch at every station, her book forgotten on her lap. When at last the engine pulled in to Waterloo, she hurried through the barriers and headed for the Underground, her mind in a whirl. Was this the worst idea she'd ever had, meeting Mac at Ruth's grave like this?

She forced herself to recall what Mac looked like. Summoning him to her mind brought Ruth back too, her eyes wide and alarmed as Rhi had yelled at the two of them.

How could you and Mac do this to Alex, Ruth. . .?
I can't believe you're my sister. . .

Rhi flinched at the memory. That was the last time she'd seen Mac. Her parents had kept her well away from the inquest that followed the accident. Would she recognize him? She knew that she would. For all her efforts, that terrible argument was as fresh in her mind as if it had happened yesterday.

The familiarity of the street when she emerged from the Underground half an hour later took her breath away. The buses, the taxis, the shop awnings, the pavements awash with people: she paused briefly, drinking it all in. Much as she loved Heartside Bay, this area had been her home for more than twelve years. Terrible things had happened here, but good things too. She let herself remember the good things. The first time she rode a bike in the park. A class prize presented in the high street library. Herself as a seven-year-old bridesmaid in a red satin dress. She had loved that dress.

She could have found St Joseph's by the Gate blindfolded. The graves were as neatly tended as ever as Rhi made her way through the churchyard, trailing her fingers over the tops of the headstones: some rough, some smooth.

As she rounded the corner of the church, she stopped dead.

The boy by Ruth's grave looked round. Rhi stared in disbelief at his brown hat. His wheelchair. This weak, pale boy – the boy she had seen at the pensioners' wedding, and at the Heartbeat Café – this wasn't Mac. Mac had been tall. Smiling. Tanned and handsome. Not . . . not. . .

"Hello Rhi," he said nervously.

As soon as Rhi heard his voice, she knew. But he looked so fragile in his chair, hunched and thin. As if he'd suffered in ways she couldn't begin to imagine. She never would have recognized him by sight alone.

"I'm so sorry for writing to you, and emailing you, and showing up in your life. But I had to speak to you. I have to tell you the truth. I'm asking you as humbly as I can. Will you listen to me?"

"You killed my sister," Rhi spat. Her voice sounded harsh, even to her own ears. "Why should I listen to anything you have to say? I should never have come. I should never have arranged this."

She turned and walked away, stumbling slightly on the tussocky grass that filled the spaces between the gravestones. *Fly with me, Rhi. . .*

Mac had taken Ruth away from her. Nothing could change that. But Rhi found her footsteps slowing as she approached the gate that led back to the street, the Tube, the railway station and the sanity of home. She had arranged this meeting to learn the truth Mac had promised her. She had to know. And perhaps . . . perhaps Mac had to know her side of the story too. She couldn't carry it alone any more.

Mac was still by Ruth's grave, his head bowed over his hands when Rhi returned. His face blazed with relief. Rhi sat down at the bench which backed on to the cool stone wall of the church.

"Start talking," she said.

Mac began haltingly. "I loved your sister, Rhi. And she loved me. We hadn't planned to fall for each other, but we did. I'm not sorry about that. She was the best thing that ever happened to me."

Rhi clenched her fists on her lap and ordered herself to keep listening.

"I was single – had been for a few months. But Ruth

was still going out with Alex." Mac swallowed. "She didn't want us to sneak around behind his back, but she was frightened of what Alex might do if she told him she wanted to break up with him. He wasn't a very stable person."

Rhi had a sudden memory of Alex shouting at Ruth outside the house one evening, after dropping her home from a date. Her sister's boyfriend had been larger than life. He'd had a temper and got jealous easily, she remembered. He knew how to make big gestures, though. Roses used to arrive at the house, and love letters, and balloons. At twelve, Rhi had thought Alex the most romantic, most handsome boy she'd ever met. She'd envied her sister, and longed for a boyfriend just like Alex. How stupid she had been.

Tears streaked Mac's cheeks. "Ruth was scared of Alex. He was very controlling. She couldn't speak to other boys without him breathing fire down her neck, shouting at her and accusing her of being unfaithful. He smothered her. She used to come to my house and cry in my room about it. She loved *me*, Rhi. But she didn't know how to break it to Alex."

Rhi's nails were biting into her palms of her hands.

"Then Alex found out." Mac's voice was so quiet now, Rhi could hardly hear him. "He tracked me down, and drove me off the road. Ruth was in the car with him. We both lost control and rolled down the bank . . . and Alex and Ruth hit the tree head-on. There was nothing I could do. I'd had a couple of drinks that night – not much, but more than Alex. I shouldn't have been driving. I have tortured myself in prison for two years thinking about that. I might have lost the use of my legs in the accident, but it didn't seem like enough. I felt like I should have died as well."

It was time, Rhi realized. Time to share her own secret.

"I've been torturing myself too," she said quietly.

Mac looked surprised. "Why?"

"When I . . ." Swallowing was surprisingly hard. "Remember when I caught you both together that morning, in Ruth's room?" She rushed on before she lost her courage. "I was so shocked. . . Alex was the only boyfriend my sister had ever had. He'd been with her for so long, it was like he was part of the family. I felt like you and Ruth had betrayed that. Later on that day, I shouted at Ruth for cheating on Alex with you. And . . . and Alex overheard."

If only she could take it back, she thought in anguish. Those terrible words she had shouted at Ruth on the stairs without knowing Alex was down in the hallway. . . *How could you and Mac do this to Alex, Ruth? He loves you!*

"He overheard, and he took Ruth in the car to find you. . . He . . . the accident. . ."

Rhi covered her face with her hands and wept until her eyes felt raw. *I can't believe you're my sister.* The last words she ever said to Ruth.

She felt Mac pressing something into her hand. A tissue. She took it a little shakily, wiped her eyes, and made herself look at him. He looked sad and tired, but lighter too somehow.

"You were just a kid, Rhi, you didn't understand. You can't blame yourself for any of this. I was a coward for not helping Ruth confront Alex with the truth. Maybe if we'd told him earlier, been honest about it . . . but there's no point in dwelling on that."

Rhi blew her nose. "You don't blame me?" she whispered.

"I'm through with blame," Mac said. "Now I'm out of prison, my family have decided to move to Canada. I'm going with them. It's time to make a fresh start. But I needed you to know the truth: that I loved Ruth, and always will. I hope you can forgive me. Maybe not now, but—"

Rhi reached out and hugged Mac mid-sentence. He felt frail in her arms.

"I forgive you," she whispered. "Will you . . . will you stay in touch, Mac? I think it will help, having someone who understands. Who loved Ruth as much as I did."

His voice sounded close to breaking. "Of course I will. Thank you, Rhi. From the bottom of my heart."

SEVENTEEN

Rhi walked slowly back to the Tube, her mind full of all the things Mac had told her. Ruth had always been the risk-taker when she and Rhi had been younger, but that had changed. When Alex came along, Ruth had grown quieter, more cautious. More scared of the unknown. Rhi had put it down to the mysteries of growing up. Mac had talked about water fights, dares, laughter – all the things Rhi had loved best about her sister that she thought had gone for ever. It seemed that Ruth hadn't "grown up" at all. She'd simply lost herself in Alex, and found herself again in Mac.

Rhi understood now how Alex had been the wrong person for Ruth. How had she never seen that before? A good relationship brought out the best in a person.

It didn't make that person somehow less than they'd been before.

As she waited on the Tube platform, Rhi thought about her and Max. He had made her less of a person, with his cheating and his phoney charm. She had become more hesitant, less inclined to follow her instincts and quicker to believe herself in the wrong. With Brody . . . she felt bigger. Like she was truly in charge of her own destiny.

Rhi realized with a jerk that it was almost one o'clock. The wedding reception started at two. The very last train she could catch was the ten past one. If she missed it, she wouldn't get to the Heartbeat on time to play their set and Brody would be left to perform by himself. The things Mac had told her had put the wedding completely out of her head. How could she have forgotten?

She sat tensely on the edge of her seat as the Tube rocked and swayed into the mainline station. Taking the escalator two steps at a time, Rhi flew on to the concourse, and anxiously scanned the departures board. Which platform did she need?

No sooner had she spotted the information on the

board than it disappeared. The concourse clock ticked over ten past one. Rhi watched her train depart with absolute dismay. *I've missed it*, she thought. She sat down on the bench opposite the gates. *Brody will think I did it on purpose. . .*

"Miss the ten past, did you?" A guard was smiling kindly at her.

Rhi nodded. "When's the next one?" she asked, dreading the answer.

"In an hour's time, love."

Rhi groaned and buried her face in her hands. She had lost track of the time so badly. The poor couple getting married today wouldn't have the music they wanted, and it was all her fault.

"But if you hurry," the guard continued, "you can catch the one-fifteen to Portsmouth, change at Woking and join the train you just missed."

Rhi sprinted down the concourse and threw herself on to the train the guard had suggested. By half past one, connection safely made, she was rattling towards Heartside Bay on the train, out of breath and seriously relieved.

Talking to Mac had made her realize something

very important. Something she needed to tell Brody, preferably before they were due to perform. She bit her nails and watched the sea glimmer into view on the horizon. The train journey had never felt so long.

The moment the train pulled into the station, Rhi was running like a hare towards her locker. She wrenched out her guitar and wedding bag and sprinted towards the Heartbeat Café. She had to get there before they were due to sing or she'd lose her chance.

Brody looked up as Rhi flew through the stage door, red-faced and panting.

"Brody!" she gasped, holding her side. "Brody, I'm so, so sorry. I missed the train—"

"It's OK, you're here and that's all that matters. I thought I was going to have to do it by myself." He paused. "Wait, what train?"

"Brody, I have to talk to you. Stay there." Rhi grabbed her wedding outfit – a bright pink dress and a small green hat Polly had customized for her with ribbons and feathers – and ran for the toilets. She had never changed so fast in her life.

"I'm still here," said Brody, smiling at her as she raced backstage again. "Rhi, I'm so glad you came.

I thought you wouldn't show up after . . . you know. Everything. I should have known better."

He looked so handsome standing there in his best blue shirt. Rhi's heart was full to bursting. She caught his hands and pulled him towards her.

"I've just been to London," she said.

He looked startled. "No wonder you look out of breath. What was going on in London?"

"It doesn't matter," said Rhi. "What matters is what happens now. You complete me, Brody Baxter. There's no point in fighting it. I want to be with you, whatever it takes. We'll work through your alcohol addiction together. I've been very blind, and stupid and judgemental, and very slow, and very, very scared. I'm not any more. Can you . . . will you forgive me?'

Brody's face lit up. "Can *I* forgive you?" he said incredulously. He pulled her towards him, lacing his fingers through hers. "Rhi, there's nothing to forgive."

Rhi put her arms around his neck and gazed into his eyes. She wanted to remember this moment. *Ruth the risk-taker would approve*, she thought. She could hardly believe she was doing this, or how good it felt.

"Someone forgave me today for something that

I once did," she told him. "Something I am very ashamed of. I'm not perfect, Brody. No one is. It's stupid to hold you up to the kind of standard that doesn't exist. The only thing we can do is be the best people we can be." She looked intently at him. It was important that he understood. "You make me the best person I can be. You complete me, Brody." And she brought his face to hers and kissed him on the lips.

In a flash Brody's arms came tightly around her, lifting her off her feet. The kiss was everything Rhi had imagined it would be: deep and fierce and wonderful. She wanted it to go on for ever. . .

Someone was announcing something.

"Ladies and gentlemen, it gives me great pleasure to present . . . Rhi Wills and Brody Baxter!"

The stage curtain swished open. An instant later, Rhi and Brody sprang apart in surprise and looked out at a sea of faces gazing up at them on the stage.

"Hello," said Rhi a little weakly.

There was a burst of laughter and applause. "Kiss her again!" someone shouted from the back of the room.

Brody's arms were still around Rhi's waist. He

leaned into the microphone. "If you insist," he said, grinning. He bent his head and kissed Rhi again so that she felt it in the tips of her toes. The roar from the audience this time was even louder.

"Ready to sing now?" Brody enquired, pulling back and looking into Rhi's eyes.

The bubble of happiness inside Rhi threatened to lift her off the stage completely. "Never readier," she said.

EIGHTEEN

Rhi sang better than she'd ever sung before, her head resting against Brody's as they played their set for the wedding. Every song they performed was met with an enormous cheer. The bride and groom even stood on their table to applaud at the end. Rhi took her bow, holding tightly on to Brody's hand. She was in some kind of dream, and she never wanted to wake up.

The moment they were off the stage, Brody was kissing her again. "You were sensational out there today," he said, hugging her close.

"I wonder why?" Rhi teased.

For that she got another kiss. "Are you busy tomorrow?" he asked when they broke apart. "Can we go out?"

"Are you asking me on a date, Brody Baxter?"

He laughed. "Yes I am, Rhiannon Wills. Meet me at the clock tower tomorrow at ten?"

Rhi hugged him, curling her fingers through his hair. "Wild horses wouldn't keep me away," she promised.

Sunday morning dawned bright and sunny. Rhi found herself singing in the bathroom as she brushed her teeth. It was amazing how different she felt to the previous day.

Sometimes you have to do the thing you're scared of, she thought, recalling her doubts about meeting Mac. *Then you won't be scared any more.*

It had done her so much good to talk with Mac the way she had. She still felt guilty about her part in the accident, but now the pain was shared it didn't seem to hurt as much. Now she felt like she had wings. Wings that would fly her all the way to the clock tower, to meet a boy with blond hair and blue eyes who made her heart melt.

Brody was at the clock tower just as he'd promised, his head bent over the strings of his guitar as he plucked out a tune, flip-flops on his feet and his favourite beaded necklace around his neck. Rhi felt a tiny flip of nerves in her stomach. She'd hate it if the magic of yesterday had gone. If Brody had decided in the clear morning light that he would listen to his AA sponsor and not date her after all.

She hesitated, watching him for a moment. She loved the way his fingers moved so deftly over the guitar strings. She loved . . . him.

The moment he saw her, he was on his feet, setting his guitar down at the base of the clock tower and striding towards her with a wide smile on his face. Rhi felt the relief of his arms coming round her, and his lips pressing down on hers. She kissed him back joyfully, for what felt like a very long time.

"Hello," he said, coming up for air.

Rhi had such a stupid grin on her face she could hardly speak. "Hello yourself," she managed, before he started kissing her again.

They walked together on the beach, hand in hand, stopping every few minutes to kiss each other. They climbed along the bottom of the cliffs and sat curled up together with their backs against the warm rocks. Brody played his guitar, and Rhi sang.

"The mermaids are listening," Brody told her as

they reached the end of a song, raising his voice over the crash of the sea against the shore.

"Right," said Rhi, rolling her eyes.

"I'm serious," he insisted. "Look over there, you might see them."

Rhi looked towards the low-lying rocks near the shore that he was pointing at. She sat up very straight as she glimpsed a dark, wet head swimming in the water. "Oh my gosh," she said, startled almost beyond words.

The "mermaid" flopped out of the water and settled down to sunbathe on the warm rocks. Rhi gaped with a combination of amazement and disappointment, then shoved Brody in the side. "You said it was a mermaid!" she accused, laughing.

"Seals *are* mermaids. Did no one ever tell you that?"

Rhi looked at the seal's ugly, friendly face with its bristling whiskers and blubbery brown body. It was adorable, but hardly beautiful.

"Are you telling me sailors fell in love with *seals*?" she said.

"You need to sing more sweetly for the pretty ones to come along," Brody said, laughing.

"You'll pay for that," Rhi joked, pushing him back so that he lay flat on the rock they were sitting on.

"What are you going to do? Tickle me to death?"

Rhi snuggled down beside him. "Kiss you to death, more like."

With the warmth of the sun on their backs, it was easy to lose track of time. The seal grew bored of its rock and slid soundlessly back into the sea.

"Hungry?" Brody inquired. When Rhi nodded, he grinned. "I have an idea."

They busked in the town centre for an hour, earning enough for two generous portions of fish and chips, which they ate with their legs dangling over the end of the pier.

"We should do this every day," Brody said, dipping his chips in Rhi's ketchup.

"School would get in the way," Rhi pointed out.

"Me and classrooms never got on," Brody admitted. "I knew early on that music would be my future. Are you going to stay on after GCSEs?"

"Mum wants me to."

"What do *you* want?"

"I want to finish my education, but I want to make my life in music. Best of both worlds."

"Good plan."

It *was* a good plan, Rhi reflected that night as she lay in bed and thought about her perfect day with Brody. If only her mother could see it that way. She drifted away to sleep, thinking of seals and mermaids, ketchup, kisses and music. Always music.

"Results!" Mr Morrison announced at school the following morning. "Try to contain your excitement, class. Any questions, I'll be happy to answer."

"I can't look," Lila groaned as their form teacher laid two pieces of paper on her and Rhi's desks. "Rhi, can you read them out for me? My parents will kill me if I've failed anything, provided Josh hasn't killed me first. As long as I've passed everything, I'll be fine. Please tell me I'm going to be fine."

"As, Bs and a D," Rhi said, scanning Lila's results sheet.

Lila sat up. "I got a *D*?" she said. "In what?"

"Whatever happened to 'I'll be fine as long as I've passed everything'?" Rhi enquired. Pushing her hair out of her eyes, she took up her own sheet. C, C, B, C. . . Not great, but at least they were passes. Her eye moved further down the sheet.

She'd got an F for geography.

Her mother was waiting for her when she got in from school, eyes sparking with rage. She waved her phone under Rhi's nose.

"What is this?"

Rhi found she was feeling strangely reckless. "A phone," she said calmly.

"Don't get fresh with me. The school texted me your results. An *F*?"

"I passed the rest," Rhi said, setting her bag down by the door.

"Bs and Cs might technically be passes, Rhi, but you'll never get anywhere in life with those. And the *F* . . . I can't begin to tell you how disappointed I am. Did nothing I said to you sink in?"

"Mum, they aren't GCSEs, they're just school exams—"

"Just school exams? Rhi, your teachers will use these results to predict your GCSEs!"

"I will study harder for my GCSEs, OK? I promise. But these—"

"I don't want to hear it," Rhi's mother began.

"You never want to hear anything, do you?" Rhi shouted. "Never! When are you going to understand that I don't *want* the life you've mapped out for me, Mum? I want a career in music, with Brody! We're going places already. We're booked solid all summer, we've even had to turn down gigs! We have a massive following on the internet and it's growing all the time. Why can't you hear what I'm telling you? Why can't you be proud of me? I'm not Ruth, Mum! I'm me! Look. . ." She hurried into her mother's study and typed her name into the search engine that stood open on the computer screen. "I'll show you. I'll prove it to you. . ."

The first video that popped up surprised Rhi. She didn't think anyone had been filming that night. She stared at herself on the stage at the Heartbeat.

"*This is a song called 'With You By Myself'. I wrote it for my sister. Ruth died two years ago now, but she's right here in the song. At least, she—*"

Rhi shut down the video and closed the laptop.

She wasn't ready to talk about that song with her mother. She felt defeated. All the good things that had happened to her lately suddenly felt like a long time ago.

"Forget it. You'll never understand."

"Rhi, come back here!" her mother shouted after her as she ran up the stairs to her room. "We need to talk about this!"

Rhi grabbed clothes, throwing them heedlessly into a bag. "No," she said, picking up her guitar and coming back down the stairs, pushing past her mother in the hallway and opening the front door. "*You* need to *listen*."

"Where do you think you're going?"

"To live with Dad!"

Slamming the door felt intensely satisfying. Rhi moved as fast as she could, half running and half walking, desperate to get away. Her dad would make room for her in the flat. She'd sleep on the sofa, she'd sleep anywhere but back at the house. She couldn't live with her mother any more. It was too hard.

Her case was heavy. With her guitar bumping on her back, Rhi took the stairs up to her father's flat and banged on the door. It creaked open all by itself.

"Dad, I *have* to live with you," she implored, barging in. "Mum—"

The words died in her throat. Her father was kissing a stranger on his sofa.

NINETEEN

Rhi felt as if her feet were frozen to the floor. Her father and another woman. A woman who wasn't her mother. A woman she'd never seen before.

This isn't possible. This is not happening.

Her father leaped to his feet. Rhi looked at the woman on the sofa, who had clapped her hands over her mouth in horror and was now gazing at Rhi over the tops of her fingers with wide, dark eyes. If it hadn't been so shocking, it would have been funny.

Rhi suddenly realized she *had* seen the woman before, painting a bowl of fruit in her dad's art class. She'd been the one touching her father on the arm, like she owned him. Her eyes darted sideways to the easel propped up beneath the skylight by the kitchen.

The painting her father had covered up the last time she was here was visible now. The same woman's wide dark eyes looked out at the room. Everything was becoming horribly clear.

Her father was walking towards her, his arms held out. "Rhi, I'm so sorry, I never meant for you to find out like this—"

Rhi flattened herself against the door frame. "Don't come near me," she hissed. *Mum*, she thought in anguish.

Her father stayed where he was, looking pleadingly at her. "It's important for you to understand, Rhi. Please listen to—"

"This is why you didn't want me moving in, isn't it?" Rhi cut in. Anger was descending like a heavy sea fog, making it hard to think straight. "You didn't want me to find out your dirty little secret."

Her father looked like he had been slapped. "I. . . Your mother and I broke up, Rhi. I didn't start anything until afterwards—"

Rhi tipped her chin jerkily at the woman on the sofa, who still hadn't moved. "Is *she* the reason you destroyed our family?"

"Rhi, our family was broken long ago. You know that. We've talked about this."

"You never mentioned *her*, though, did you?" Rhi's legs were shaking. She could hardly bear to look at her father. "How long has it been going on, Dad?"

"Not long, Rhi, please believe me. . ."

Why did everyone always say that to her? Why should she believe her father when he'd never said a word about meeting someone else?

"You were *kissing* her!" Rhi shouted. "You left barely a week ago, Dad. Don't tell me this has all happened in just one week! I'm not a child, I don't believe you any more. I don't believe anything you say."

The woman had stood up now. "Hello Rhi," she said nervously. "I'm Laura. I've heard so much about you."

The fog of anger was blinding Rhi now. "Well I've heard nothing about you," she said coolly. "I'm not interested in anything *she* has to say," she said, switching her gaze back to her father. "Tell her to go away."

She sounded like her mother, she realized. She didn't care.

The woman gave a sob and fled past Rhi, out of the door and down the stairs. Rhi's father stayed where he was as the door down at ground level banged hard.

"Rhi," he tried again, "please try to understand. None of this is Laura's fault. Your mother and I – our relationship has been over for years. Laura's an artist, she understands me in ways your mother never could. We never meant to hurt you. Life goes on, darling. We have to make the best of what we have."

Rhi could feel her heart contracting in her chest. Slowly squeezing down to a small, hard nugget of stone.

"You know what, Dad?" she said. "I'm past caring. You chose her over us and that's all I need to know. You and Mum are the most selfish people I've ever met. I have no home any more. I have no family. I lost it all when Ruth died."

"Rhi, don't say that—"

Rhi sprinted away down the stairs and out into the street, clinging to her guitar and her bag. They were all she had left. She ran through the old town, sobbing and gasping. She needed somewhere to go. . .

Any time you want to escape, you can come here,

OK? It's really important to have a space where you can just – be.

Polly.

Rhi wanted to cry at the thought of Polly's calm, bright, welcoming home. Polly would understand. She had known it would be like this. She had even warned Rhi about it.

Rhi swerved up Polly's road. Sweat was pouring down her face. She could feel blisters forming on the palms of her hand from her guitar and her bag.

Polly opened the door before Rhi had even reached the doorbell. Rhi found herself wrapped up in Polly's embrace, held and rocked on the doorstep.

"Dad. . . Mum. . ." Rhi choked in Polly's arms. "He. . . I caught Dad with someone else. Polly, I don't think I can stand it—"

"It's OK," Polly soothed. "Breathe, Rhi. You're going to be fine. Just breathe. . ."

Rhi tried to get herself under control. She sobbed more hopelessly than ever. Had it really been just yesterday that she had been so happy with Brody at the beach? So much had happened in just a week. Mum, Dad, Mac . . . Laura. She cried until she couldn't cry any more. Then at last, feeling as weak as a kitten, she let Polly bring her inside and sit her down at the kitchen table.

"You need some sweet tea," said Polly. "For the shock. They always do that in the movies. I think sweet tea is vile, personally."

Rhi gave a weak laugh. "Tea would be nice," she said. She was going to cry again, she could feel it.

The tea was disgusting, but soothing at the same time. Rhi wrapped her hands around the mug and bowed her head over the sweet steam.

"It will get better," said Polly, watching her.

Rhi groaned. "I saw him kissing this other woman, Polly. It was the freakiest thing ever."

Polly grimaced. "That must have been bad.'

Rhi felt sick just thinking about it. "Polly, can I stay here?" she blurted. "I don't have anywhere else."

"Of course you can," Polly said. "Listen, Mum's got some chocolate biscuits hidden somewhere. She's on a healthy eating lark, apparently, but she keeps a stash for moments like this."

Three biscuits later, Rhi was starting to feel a little more normal. Even a tiny bit ashamed of her behaviour. She of all people had seen how unhappy her father had been lately. Wasn't it a good thing that he'd met someone who understood him at last? She wished she could feel happy for him, but all she could think about was how her mother was going to react when she found out. She was *bound* to find out. Like Eve had said, Heartside Bay was a small town. Rhi felt like an old elastic band being pulled between her parents.

"What am I going to do?" she moaned, resting her head on the table between her hands.

"You're going to tell me about Brody," said Polly.

Rhi jerked her head up. "You know about Brody?"

"Ollie and I saw you kissing by the clock tower yesterday," Polly beamed.

"Don't tell the others," Rhi begged, feeling embarrassed. "This is still really new for us. I want to enjoy it a bit longer without any gossip, you know?"

"Cross my heart," Polly said. She looked misty-eyed. "You look so adorable together. When did it happen?"

Rhi's heart lightened. "We got together on Saturday," she said shyly. "He's so wonderful, Polly. He understands me. I'm a better person when I'm with him."

As Rhi said the words, she realized her father had said something similar to her about Laura, but she'd been too angry to listen. *She understands me in ways your mother never could. . .* Was this something else she ought to learn? That she was no different from her father?

"What?" said Polly, watching her.

Rhi shook her head. She needed to think that one through by herself first. "Nothing," she said aloud. "Do you want the last biscuit?"

They both heard the car wheels screeching up outside the house. Someone sounded like they were in a hurry. Rhi followed Polly curiously to the door as Polly flipped the latch.

Lila's dad was standing on the doorstep in full police uniform.

"Hello, Polly. Is Rhi here?"

Rhi realized she had started screaming. It was the day Ruth had died all over again. Police cars, uniformed officers on the doorstep. The end of life as she had known it. The end of everything. It was happening again. It was. . .

She slumped sideways into darkness.

TWENTY

Someone was sponging her forehead. Rhi stirred, lifting her hand to push them away.

"No," she mumbled. Her head felt cold. "Ruth. . ."

Warm hands took her fingers and held them. She heard her name called from somewhere far away.

"Rhi? Please wake up, Rhi!'

Rhi opened her eyes groggily. Polly was beside her, anxiously sponging her forehead. Over by the door, Chief Murray of the Heartside Bay Police stood with his cap in his hands. A faint sense of panic stirred her again.

"Where am I?" she mumbled. "What happened?"

"I didn't meant to frighten you when I appeared like that, Rhi," Chief Murray said apologetically. "There's nothing to worry about, nothing bad has happened. Your parents called me, asking if I could find you. They were worried about where you'd gone, that was all. I spoke to Lila and she suggested here. How are you feeling?"

Rhi sat up. "A bit stupid," she said weakly.

Polly put the sponge down and hugged her. "You gave me such a fright," she said a little tearfully. "One minute you were standing there and the next minute you were on the floor. Chief Murray helped me to carry you in here."

Rhi looked at Chief Murray. "So . . . everything's OK? There hasn't. . ." She swallowed. "There hasn't been another accident?"

The chief of police shook his head. "Just two worried parents. I've called them to let them know you're safe."

Rhi rubbed her eyes. "Thank you," she said after a moment.

She should have called when she had got to Polly's. Of course her parents would have been worried. After losing Ruth, her mother in particular always wanted to know where Rhi was. Her fussing had annoyed Rhi on countless occasions, but she suddenly found that she understood. She was all her parents had left.

She took out her phone and dialled home. Her mother answered on the first ring.

"Rhi? Thank goodness you're safe. You are safe, aren't you?"

"I'm safe, Mum," Rhi assured her. "I just needed. . ." She remembered Polly's phrase. "I just needed space to think."

"I had your father on the phone, beside himself about an argument you'd had, wanting to know if you were with me. But of course we'd argued too, so you weren't here. We were so worried. . . It was *thoughtless* of you not to let us know where you were!" Through the anger, Rhi could detect acute relief in her mother's voice. Even a flash of love. "Promise me you'll never disappear like that again."

"I promise," she said. "I was mad at you, but I didn't mean to scare you, Mum."

"Are you coming home?"

Her mother sounded strangely vulnerable. Rhi thought about her bag and guitar, still sitting in Polly's hallway. She thought about her father and Laura and the little flat, and her mother all alone, clutching the phone to her ear.

"Yes," she said quietly. "I'm coming home."

"I'm passing that way, I can drop you back," Chief Murray offered as Rhi slid her phone into her pocket.

"Thank you, Chief Murray. And thanks for everything else, Polly," she said, looking at her friend. "For listening."

Polly hugged her. "Any time."

It wasn't far from Polly's house to her own. Rhi sat in the back of the police car with her guitar in her lap. Her parents were both waiting in the door when Chief Murray swung up by the front gate. Rhi watched them both hurry down to the gate to meet her. Her mother pull her into a hard hug.

"You'll be the death of me, Rhiannon Wills," she said fiercely.

Rhi smiled against her mother's jacket. "I'll try not to be."

Her father hovered beside her, looking unsure whether to hug her or not. Rhi put him out of his misery and hugged him first.

"We all need tea and toast," her mother announced loudly. "Unless you have any better ideas, Patrick."

"Whatever you say, Anita."

Rhi sat at the kitchen table and watched her parents dancing politely around each other. She appreciated the way they weren't shouting for once. It didn't seem fair to tell them she was already full of tea and biscuits from Polly's house.

Toast made and mugs filled, her parents sat opposite her at the table. Rhi caught the way they glanced at each other.

"What?" she said warily.

Her mother stirred her tea with a little more vigour than necessary. "I saw the video," she said. "The song you wrote about Ruth."

Rhi blanched. "You did?"

"I heard it when you sang it at the Heartbeat," her father put in. "Your mother said you'd pulled it up on the computer for her this afternoon."

"And then you shut it down," her mother added. She looked uncomfortable. "I opened it again when you left. The introduction . . . well. Let's say it caught my attention."

Rhi could feel her throat tightening. "And?" she said nervously. "What did you think?"

Her mother's eyes shone weirdly. Rhi realized they were full of tears. "I thought it was beautiful," she said. "You based it on those times in the playground, didn't you?"

Her mother *remembered*? "Ruth always dared me to swing high," Rhi whispered. "It was scary, but it made me feel alive. *She* made me feel alive."

"She had that effect on us too," said her father.

Rhi couldn't quite believe they were having this conversation. Talking about Ruth. It was as if they'd had an unspoken agreement on the subject that somehow wasn't there any more.

"Do you remember when Ruth jumped into the river after her ball, Patrick?" said her mother suddenly. She had an odd, faraway look in her eyes. "Rhi, you were too young to remember this, but we were walking along the river when she dropped her ball in the water. She was waist deep in the water before I had blinked. Thank goodness the river was shallow. She was a daredevil, that one."

"She was only about five," said Rhi's dad. "Or was it six?"

"Six. The ball was a birthday present from Auntie June."

A red ball floating among some ducks. Ruth's green dress covered in river weeds.

"It was red," Rhi blurted. "The ball. Wasn't it?"

Her parents looked astonished.

"You do remember!" her mother exclaimed.

Rhi laughed, partly out of shock. "Yes. I cried."

"I don't remember that," said her father. "You were always a stoical little thing in those ridiculous bunches your mother put in your hair."

"They weren't ridiculous, they were adorable," said her mother. She sipped her tea. "Ruth put glue in them once."

There was magic in the air. Rhi could feel it. Ruth was peeping around the kitchen door, laughing along with them as the memories started pouring out. If she turned around, she might glimpse her from the corner of her eye. She didn't dare to move.

"You know I went to London on Saturday?" she said quietly. "I went to Ruth's grave. I met someone there. Mac – Chris McAllister, the boy whose car was involved in Ruth's accident. He wrote to me.

Remember the letter you found in my room, Mum? That was him. He wanted to tell me something about the day the accident happened."

Her parents both looked as if they'd been turned to stone. Rhi forged on.

"He told me things about that day that I'd never understood. About him and Ruth and how they loved each other and how scared they were of telling Alex. And I . . . I told Mac things too. About how I had blurted out that I'd seen him kissing Ruth when Alex was listening, and how Alex had gone looking for him in the car. . ." Rhi was trembling hard. She wasn't sure she could continue.

Her mother reached across the table and took her hand. "Rhi, you were twelve years old. There were lots of things about that day that you couldn't have understood."

"I blame myself," Rhi said miserably. "Alex wouldn't have taken Ruth out to look for Mac if I hadn't said what I'd said. I know . . . I know you'll never forgive me. I'm sorry."

Her parents exchanged a long, wordless look.

"Rhi, your mother and I reconciled ourselves to

what happened a long time ago," said her father gently. "It was a tragic accident, a chain of events that we can't change. We should have talked to you about it at the time, but we were all in too much pain. Your mother and I don't blame you. We love you."

Rhi wiped her eyes, which had filled with tears.

"You can be very silly sometimes, Rhiannon," said her mother, in the brisk tone she used to cover up her emotions. "We both love you very much. Your father has offered to let you live with him for a while, if it would help you get used to the idea of this divorce. I don't want to lose you, but keeping you here with me might do just that."

"I'd like to have you," said her father. He looked intently at Rhi. "If you'd like to come."

"Yes, I'd like that very much," Rhi found herself saying. "Very much."

TWENTY-ONE

Rhi groaned and straightened up with her hands on her back. The box of shoes had been heavy. Moving all her stuff into her dad's flat was proving to be a tough workout. She must have walked up and down the long flight of stairs to the top of the building at least twenty times already that morning, and it was only half past ten.

"You look about a hundred and three when you do that back-stretching thing," Brody observed, a large box of books in his arms.

Rhi giggled, and wiped her forehead with the back of her hand. "Shut up and put my books by the window, will you?"

"Your slave obeys," said Brody, and set the books down where Rhi had indicated.

Rhi draped her arms around his neck as he stood up again. "And what would my slave like in return?" she teased.

Brody's blue eyes shone with laughter. "A kiss from my lady," he said. "And less flogging."

"The pyramids didn't build themselves, you know," said Rhi.

Brody brushed her hair from her face and kissed her by the light of the little window with its view of Heartside Bay's rooftops. Rhi gave a sigh of contentment and turned in the circle of his arms to admire her little room. It was small, admittedly, but it was adorable. One of the first things she'd done was hang up the picture of her, Ruth and their parents laughing in Trafalgar Square. It sat against the white walls like a small and glowing jewel. There were no curtains yet, but Polly had promised to help her make some very soon. *Yellow*, Rhi thought, imagining them blowing in the breeze over her little white bed. *A happy colour.*

Her father staggered into the room with an enormous box.

"Where do you want this, Rhi?" he puffed.

Rhi didn't remember a box that large. "That's not mine," she said, mystified. "Where did you get it?"

"Take it from me, will you? Before I drop it!"

Brody moved to lift the box from her father's arms, but Rhi beat him to it. She staggered back slightly as her father let go with a wink. The box was as light as air.

"There's nothing in it!" she said indignantly.

"Good joke though," her father said, grinning. "I had a whole load of new canvases delivered yesterday in that thing. You could probably build a house with it."

It was hard to resist her father when he was in this kind of jokey mood. She hadn't seen him this carefree in months. Rhi put the box down and rested her hands on her hips as Brody laughed loud and long.

"Ruth had a box like that once," she said, unable to resist a smile. "She painted it red and gave it windows. We played with it until it fell down."

Her father looked delighted at the memory. "If there was a little more space around here, you could make a playhouse of your own. Tea break?"

The flat was looking much tidier than the last time

Rhi had been here. As she and Brody sat at the small kitchen table with its red tablecloth and vase of yellow and white daisies, she sensed a woman's touch in the arrangement of furniture, the curtains at the windows and the matching crockery by the sink. Some of her father's pictures had been mounted and hung around the living room, the pebble still life and the seagull among them. They had been hung with care and attention, like the hanger knew which space would bring out the best in which picture.

"Penny for them?" said Brody, reaching across the tablecloth to hold Rhi's hand as she finished her tea.

"I was just thinking how homely this place looks. I think Dad's found someone who understands him at last. I know what that's like," Rhi added shyly.

"I'll fetch some more boxes," said her dad, heading for the door to the flat. "Back in a minute."

Brody pulled Rhi to her feet. "Some more kisses needed, I think."

Rhi wondered if she'd ever get tired of kissing Brody. He was such a lovely height and shape. *We fit together like . . . like an A major chord.* Rhi grinned to herself, pleased with her comparison.

The front door banged back on its hinges. Rhi turned to face her friends, resting the side of her face against Brody's shirt.

"Whew, those are some stairs," Lila panted, holding her sides. "We're all going to get really fit coming to visit you." Her eyes widened at the sight of Brody and Rhi with their arms around each other. "I knew it!" she hooted. "I knew you two would get together in the end!"

Eve whistled. "You really were a romance waiting to happen. Adorable. Simply adorable."

Behind Eve, Polly winked at Rhi. She had kept Rhi's secret, just as she'd promised. But Rhi was through with secrets now. She smiled at her friends as Brody squeezed her around the waist.

"We do our best," she laughed.

Rhi's dad staggered into the flat again with one shoebox in his arms. "This one almost broke me in half," he announced, smirking. "I swear, it weighs more than this whole building put together."

Later that night the Heartbeat Café was packed. Even the roof garden, usually the preserve of the brave few who didn't mind walking up and down the stairs to fetch food and drink, was full of people crammed on to benches, enjoying the views far out across the glittering sea.

Backstage, Brody ran his thumb tenderly across Rhi's cheek.

"Ready to sing?" he asked.

The cheer was deafening as they stepped hand in hand into the spotlight, their guitars around their necks. Rhi blinked at the crowd in astonishment. Even by the usual Saturday night standards, it was busy tonight.

She saw her friends crammed around the usual table, clapping louder than anyone else in the room. HEARTBEAT SUMMER SPECTACULAR! screamed a large banner slung across the ceiling. There was red and white bunting looped around the walls, and yellow and blue balloons everywhere. Almost every table held a huge pitcher of fruit punch, heavy with ice and mint. MINT PUNCH: FREE PITCHER WITH EVERY SUMMER SANDWICH PLATTER! was scrawled across the blackboard behind her father's head at the bar. The idea of free punch had Eve's style stamped all over it.

Eve could spot a business opportunity like a cat spots a mouse.

"Loving the punch idea, Eve," Rhi called down from the stage, grinning.

Hand in hand with her girlfriend Becca, Eve raised her glass. "Don't thank me," she drawled. "Thank all those lovely free mint plants currently running wild in the roof garden. I think your father ran out of sandwiches half an hour ago."

"Start with "Heartbreaker", Rhi!" someone shouted from the back of the room.

Rhi obliged, with Brody on harmonies. Tonight it felt as if they were more in tune with each other than ever. Their voices soared and looped together, their guitar strings blending into one sound. The crowd knew most of the songs, somehow – even "With Me By Myself", which Rhi performed right at the end of the show. The power of social media was an amazing thing.

"I thought I would fail," Rhi sang as the crowd swayed, "I thought I would fall, but flying alone isn't lonesome at all. . ."

"Because you aren't far, you're so very near. . ." Brody played softly beside her.

"You're deep in my heart and you won't disappear," the crowd sang. "I'm flying with you but I'm all by myself . . . I'm flying with you but I'm all by myself."

Rhi's eyes were bright with tears as she smiled at the rapturous response of the crowd. As she bowed, she caught sight of a figure in a black suit and grey shirt, standing beside her father and waving.

"Beautiful," her mother mouthed at her across the room. "I'm proud of you, Rhi. I'm so proud of you."

Rhi waved and smiled harder than ever, clutching tightly on to Brody's hand. Her mother was here, listening to her sing for the first time. It made a perfect night better than she could ever have hoped for. Her mother was proud of her.

And, somewhere, she knew that Ruth was too.

LOOK OUT FOR MORE

HEARTSIDE BAY

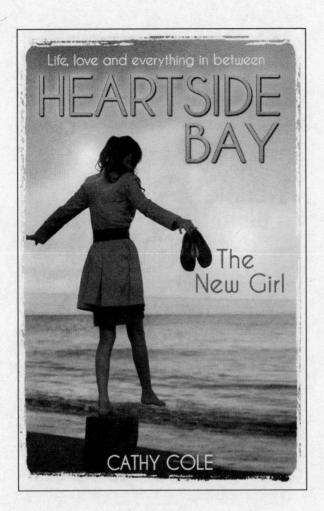

Life, love and everything in between

HEARTSIDE
BAY

The
New Girl

CATHY COLE

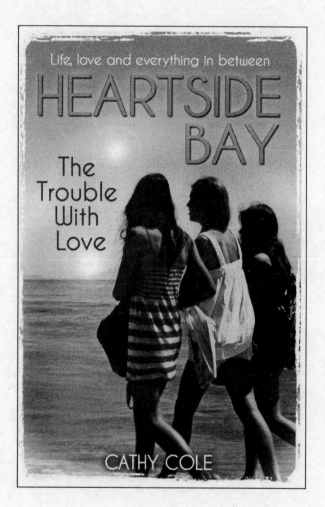

Life, love and everything in between

HEARTSIDE BAY

The Trouble With Love

CATHY COLE

Life, love and everything in between

HEARTSIDE BAY

More
Than a
Love
Song

CATHY COLE

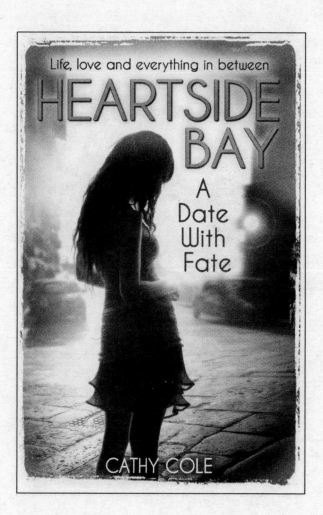

Life, love and everything in between

HEARTSIDE BAY

BAY

A Date With Fate

CATHY COLE

Life, love and everything in between

HEARTSIDE BAY

Never a Perfect Moment

CATHY COLE

Life, love and everything in between

HEARTSIDE BAY

Kiss at Midnight

CATHY COLE

Life, love and everything in between

HEARTSIDE BAY

Back to You

CATHY COLE